Gideon

KATHI S. BARTON

This is a work of fiction. Names, characters, places, and incidents are products of the author's imagination or are used fictitiously and are not to be construed as real. Any resemblance to actual events, locations, organizations, or persons, living or dead, is entirely coincidental.

World Castle Publishing, LLC
Pensacola, Florida
Copyright © Kathi S. Barton 2017
Paperback ISBN: 9781629898193
eBook ISBN: 9781629898209
First Edition World Castle Publishing, LLC, October 30, 2017
http://www.worldcastlepublishing.com

Cover: Karen Fuller
Editor: Maxine Bringenberg

Prologue

Eve sat in her chair and thought about what her life, what little there was left of it, had come to mean. It wasn't like her to feel sorry for herself, but she knew that she was going to die, and soon, and she felt that she had a right to it. When she heard someone at the door, she smiled when she spied Sally there. The young woman had been coming to the castle since she'd been born, hanging on her mother's apron like it was the life line that it was. And thankfully the child looked nothing like her beloved mother.

"Mistress, you wished to see me? If it is about the brownie that startled me, I swear to you that I meant him no harm." Eve said that wasn't it, but she knew that Sally would not hurt anyone. "Thank you, my lady."

Bidding her to come closer, the young woman did so, not once, Eve knew, worrying about what the others might think of her being in the personal chambers of the queen. Sally was as good as she had ever seen a woman be, but she could be like a bear defending her cubs when pushed. Eve knew this about her as well.

"I have a question to ask of you. A favor too should you answer me right. What do you plan for your life, my child? Is there a certain man that has come to you courting?" Sally flushed brightly and said that no, she was much too old for that. "You're not old at all, Sally. What are you, ten and eight? Less I'm betting."

"I am twenty and eight, my lady. Too old for courting. I would be set upon by men that have sired their sons and now needs someone to look after them." Sally laughed. "My mother, she shoed away such men when I was but a young thing. Now they fear that there is something about me."

"You are a wonderful person, and any man would be happy to have you as their bride." Sally flushed again and asked about the favor. "I have a man in mind for you. A good man that has the heart of a lion and the brains of a scholar. He'd not think that I was speaking of him, should he hear us, but he is a good man and will do you well to marry."

"Do you think him addled or with a sickness?" Eve laughed and said that he was of sound body and mind. "Then why would he want someone like me? I am too old to bear him children."

"You aren't, you know." Eve touched her hand to Sally's, holding her so that she could pass what she could to the young woman in the way of magic. "I have birthed my children, but I will not be able to see them grow into men."

"Why not, my lady? You seem of sound body and mind too. If you don't mind me saying." Eve nodded and said that she and King Anthony were to die, and soon. "No. That cannot be. Dragons, they live forever, and you are one of the best."

Eve told her all that she knew, holding nothing back, not even parts that she knew would upset the younger woman.

She told her of the witches that she had contacted. The other women, some of them not yet born, who were to come to her sons so long from now that it would seem as if she had lied. Eve even told her how she and her love were to pass from this world to the next, and what it would mean to their children. And that her own children would be paired with the sons Sally would have as well.

Sally sat there, her body stiff and hard. She was thinking, Eve knew, processing the information that she knew must be hard to know. When she looked at her, Eve wiped at her tears when Sally did, knowing that what she said now would be the difference in a great many lives.

"This man that you have in mind that I wed, he is important too, to all that is going to happen?" Eve told her that they both were. "Does he know about me? Your plan for us?"

"Nay, only you. And my Anthony, of course. And you must never tell him that you knew. I should like for it to go as we have hoped, without interfering with any more lives." Sally nodded. "You will have your father with you as well. He will live with you, helping you with our children. There are six of them, my own hatchlings."

"You have only to ask me, my lady, and I would gladly raise your sons as my own." Eve told her that she knew that, but they'd need each other. "I see. Nay, I do not, but I trust you with my life. You are not just my queen, my lady, but a dear person to me as well."

"Thank you, Sally. You've no idea what that means to me." Sally nodded and Eve bent to hand her the book. "In a few hours' time Anthony will bring young Jacob here to speak to him. I would wish that you read what I have here so that you can help him to better understand when the time comes."

"I can do that." She took the book and hid it deep within her skirts. Eve asked her what she was about. "I have a pocket here, in the event that I wish to carry more than my hands can hold. And with six sons to come to me and six more that I will enjoy raising as my own, I shall need bigger pockets, I think."

"Oh Sally, I wish with all my heart that I could be there for my sons, but I cannot think of another person, or better people than you and Jacob, to raise them for us. I know that you will do me proud." Sally thanked her again and left her there.

Eve wanted to be with her babes, stay with them until the time came, but she knew as surely as she was sitting there that it wouldn't help at all. When Anthony, her only reason for breathing, joined her in the big room, she held his hand as she told him that Sally would be there for them.

"I'm so happy for that. I have talked to Elbert as well. He is a very good man. Raised a wonderful child on his own." Eve agreed, and they left to survey the damage left by the magical storm. "I love you my heart."

"And I you, my blood. You and I, we will be together on the other side soon, I know this."

He nodded and held her for a moment longer, her heart breaking with the knowledge that this was the last day that they'd be together as king and queen and as man and wife.

~~~

Sally watched the couple as they took to the skies. The damage that had been done last eve was great; the deaths of some of the villagers had been sad. She watched as Helena the Black came out from behind the castle, her head bleeding and her face pale from it. Sally would not aid her, not such a woman as her. Besides, she knew what she was about and cared not if she lived or died.

Making her way back to her job, she knew that there would be no supper this night, and gathered what she could to take with her when they ran. And run they would. There were only a few things that she could take with her, mostly smaller items, but she sat in the corner and read the book, from front to back, before she left. In the end Sally stayed there, knowing that sooner rather than later she'd be set on her course for the king and queen.

"What are you about? Sitting there like you've no care in the world?" She looked at her father and smiled. "Ah, I see you have been to see the queen. And you will do this thing for her?"

"Yes, Father, I shall. I will do what I need to help them." He nodded and put a few more things in the basket that was on the large block of wood that served as a cutting board for him. "She said that we'd be cared for, should we follow the rules set forth."

"We will be. Are you ready to become a mother of so many?" She said that she was glad to have any child, but to help save the queen's would be an honor. "You're a good child, my Sally. So much unlike your mother that I am as happy as the day is long."

"Mother wasn't a good person." He said that she wasn't. "I'm sorry for that, Father. To have been with someone for so long and not feel the pang of death when she passed."

"She will be missed, yes, but not in a good way." Father smiled at her. "Young Jacob, he's a good man. You could not do better had I picked him for you meself."

Father took the few things that she had in her pockets, save the book, and told her to take what she wanted from the kitchen. That after this eve, it would be wasted. Sally wandered around the big room, careful where she looked. To have such a thing, anything that she wished from here, she wanted to make it a good choice. Wrapping her hand around the knife that she had used more than any other, she put it into her pocket and looked at her father.

"I shall pick mushrooms and herbs with this. And every time that I do, I will think of the queen and her king." Father said that was good and he left, telling her that he was going to go to their home and supply it with things. "When you return, you will talk to the king?"

"Yes. Things will be ready by then. You are to stay out of sight, my child. I do not wish you to be harmed by the goings on outside these walls. Promise me." She did and told him to be careful as well. "I shall, forevermore. When I return, you will be taken to the king and meet your husband. Make yourself presentable and make me proud of you."

She wasn't one to preen herself, but she did comb her hair and wipe at her shoes. She wasn't sure what he would expect of her, but she'd give him all that she had. Jacob...she knew little of him, but was glad for the life they would have. She could only hope that she did a good job in raising the king and queen's children.

Chapter 1

Jacob stood as still as he'd ever been as he watched Lelani laying by Sally's grave. There wasn't a bit of sound going on. It seemed to him that every creature around them had stopped even breathing. As he took a step toward her, she sat up and looked at him. Jacob asked her what she'd done.

"Done? Why nothing." She started picking up the bits of this and that which seemed to have been set up around the headstone. "I just came out to have a talk with Miss Sally. She…I knew her, you see, and I wanted to—"

"Yes, don't move." Lelani sat still, even stopped stuffing a raggedy doll into the bag she had. Turning her head slowly, she watched the creature in front of them. "His name is Bolrock. We've been chasing him for a couple of hours now. He's in a bad mood. Just stay still, honey, and mayhap he won't hurt you."

"What set him off this time?" Jacob asked her if she knew him. "I do. He's been in a bad mood his entire life, I think. Bolrock, get on with yourself. You've no rights here."

The great griffin roared at her, then looked to his left.

11

Jacob wasn't so stupid as to think that wasn't a plan to distract him, so he kept his eyes on the beast. When Lelani fell back, cursing up a storm, he asked her what was wrong. He thought for sure that she'd been maimed or hurt badly.

"She's here." He asked if it was his mate. "No, not his mate. Yours. She's here. Sally is here. I never thought to see her again. But here she is—"

"Don't be that way, child. I'm in no mood for joking with something like that." Lelani turned and looked at him and he glanced at her, still watching the griffin. "Get on back to the house. I've called in the boys. We'll get this thing gathered up and be on our way, but you stay safe."

"Jacob, Sally is standing right next to you." He felt his heart hurt for the statement, and started to tell her that he didn't want to hear such things when he heard the tinkle of laughter. "She's making fun of you too."

He turned then. Slowly. Because if she was there, he wanted to see her before she disappeared again. To be honest, he didn't know if his heart could take her leaving him again. The griffin was forgotten when he saw her. Jacob took a step toward her, a small one, fearful of what might happen if he were to rush her.

"You're really here?" She nodded and laughed again. "Sally, I'm telling you right now that if you ain't here, I'm going to be sorely upset with you. Tell me that you're not joking around with this old man."

"Jacob Benson, do I ever joke around? You tell me right now what you've been doing with yourself to have holes in your sleeves like it's summer. Not to mention, you need a haircut." Beautiful words. Her fussing at him was the best thing he'd heard in decades. Moving toward her now, his pace a little faster, he asked her what else she had seen. "I've seen that you need a good bath. When was the last time you soaked in some hot water? And those boots. You'd better have wiped them before—"

He kissed her. Then, he was so happy that he picked her up and swung her around and around. His Sally was here. And she was as real as he was. Setting her down on her feet, he didn't dare let go of her, fearful that she'd go back to where she'd come from. Jacob felt alive, more alive than he'd been in more years than he could count. He had his lady love.

The griffin roared again, Jacob had it in his head to go over to it and tell it to shut up. He had his lady wife with him again and he'd not be interrupting their time, however fleeting it was. But Lelani beat him too it.

She just walked up to the beast and smacked it on the nose as he stood there. When he whimpered, his tail between his legs, Lelani moved closer to Bolrock. Jacob was so afraid for her that he started forward.

"She has this, Jacob. Trust her." He looked at his Sally and told her that he didn't want the woman hurt. "Lelani knows what she's about. The girl has dealt with this one before."

He'd not known that, but it didn't lessen his fear for the girl. But when she slapped Bolrock again, this time harder than the last, he nearly laughed when the thing went down on his belly for her.

"You're scaring these people. What do you think you're doing?" Bolrock whimpered again. "I want you to go out and find that woman. You scared her too, you great moron. And if you hurt her, I'm going to have you for my dinner. Then we're going to talk about what you did to young Mark. You hurt him, and now he's sick as a pup. What were you thinking?"

He knew that the two of them were talking. So when Lelani looked at him and told him that the woman was to the north and that she'd sent Keion to get her, Jacob wondered if the girl, whoever she was, had fallen and hurt herself more. Lelani told the faeries and brownies that were with her all the time to go back to the house and prepare it. He thought the worst.

"She's hurt, as we were told. Bolrock told me that he wished her dead, but now that he has thought it over, he knows that he was in the wrong." Jacob asked how badly she was hurt. "Bad. In addition to her concussion and broken ribs, she cut her back. Bolrock said that she's bleeding pretty badly, but she is strong and will survive if nothing else comes upon her."

"There are many creatures out there that would take advantage of a wounded human." Lelani nodded at Sally, but said nothing as she continued. "You brought me here. You...you woke me from death, and now I'm here with my family. How did you do that? You used no magic that I can feel, Lelani."

"I don't know." Lelani looked at the tree line and then back at them. "Your sons are coming. All of them save Keion. I'm sorry about that, but the woman, she needed—"

"I'll see him. I'm here now for good?" Lelani nodded. "I am, aren't I? Here for good? I'd be so sad if I was to leave here again."

"Nay, you're here. Forever." Jacob felt his heart skip several beats as the words just spoken moved over him. "I have missed you, Lady Sally. Every day for the whole of my life, I have missed you."

"And I have you as well, Lelani."

The noise coming from the tree line had them all turning. Asher was the first one to come from the woods, then the rest en masse. As soon as he spotted them, he stopped and stared, the others bumping into him from behind. Jacob thought him to have the most comical look on his face, one that he'd forever remember.

Jed came around his brother, his face full of anger, but when Jed looked in the direction that his brother was looking, Jacob had to laugh. It was priceless to see his son so hilariously speechless. They moved to them slowly, none of them saying a word. And when Asher reached out his trembling hand and touched his mom, he sobbed like his own daughter when his momma was real to him.

"Mom? You're here. With us?" Sally nodded and cried with them. Jacob pulled out his big hanky and began to wipe at his face. To see them here, all a family again, he just couldn't hold it in any longer. And his boys, grown men for more years than he cared to think about, crying like they were, tore at his poor old heart. But when Elbert came to the circle, his big dog just sat down and stared at them. "Look, Grandda, it's Mom."

Elbert leapt up and nearly knocked Sally down. Then when he shifted, becoming the man that they loved, he held his daughter to him and sobbed as well. They were all here now, it was all that Jacob could think about. Keion joined them a few minutes later, the woman not with him.

"I need help. I'm fearful of picking her up as my beast. Not to mention, she runs when she sees me." He hugged Sally too, holding her as he finished his explanation of why he was alone. "She's screaming in pain. I found her by that alone. I'm going back to keep her safe, but we need to have someone in a truck get her."

"Gideon, you and Simeon go get the truck and the medical bag. The rest of you come on with me." Jacob nodded at his Sally when she started making plans. "Dad, you know what she's going to need in the way of medicines, correct?"

15

"Yes. We have a whole passel of herbs drying in the drying house now. You go on and get her gathered up. When you bring her home, I'll be ready." Elbert looked at Simeon, who was still standing there. "You got something to say, son?"

"What if she's the one?" His mom nodded. "No. I mean, I'm not ready yet. My house is only just started, and I don't have any idea what she needs."

Sally patted him on the cheek as she made her way by him. Jacob nearly laughed at the expression on his face, but decided that he'd not tease the boy anymore. He looked upset enough. Going back to the house with Elbert, he thought of all the things that were going on and how his lady love was here to enjoy them with him. He could not wait to introduce her to her new grandbabies.

~~~

Gracie tried to stay focused on her surroundings, but she was simply in too much pain. It was difficult for her to breathe even shallow now. She knew that she was bleeding from the wound in her back too, and that it was far worse than anything else that had been done to her person. Then there was the knot on her head.

Just as she was ready to have a seat again, just to rest, her cell phone went off. Her sister.

"Mom isn't home. I've been trying to reach her since yesterday. Where is she? I swear to you, Gracie, if she's out shopping when I wanted to, then there is going to be hell to pay." There was never any hello, how are you from her sister. "She's not answering her door. Do you suppose that she's still sleeping?"

"No, she's out having fun. I'm sure that she told you that she wasn't babysitting anymore. That she wanted to have some fun before she was too old to do it." Cora said that she had, but that didn't mean her kids. "I'm pretty sure that she's still on her cruise. So yeah, it meant your kids too. And I'm also sure that she can go shopping without your approval."

"Well, that's just flipping great. How could she do this to me? I'm standing here with my kids, and she's still roaming the countryside like she doesn't have a single obligation to me." Gracie hurt too much to listen to her sister right now, but before she could tell her she needed to go, Cora went on. "I'm telling you right now, Gracie, the two of you are going to be committed as soon as I can find you. I do not need this crap right now. They raised the dues on the club I belong to. The kids are driving me nuts. All I wanted was a few hours to myself today, and now this."

"You have a nanny. You have money to burn, as you've told me on several occasions, and I'm reasonably sure that Mom is having a good time." Cora huffed. "You're a piece of work, Cora. Let Mom do this."

"She can, so long as it doesn't inconvenience me. I was going to get my hair and nails done, Gracie. It's my treat for having the kids all week." Gracie pointed out that the nanny had them. "You're showing your jealousy again. By the way, I told William about you and how you hate me having money. He said to tell you he could spot you some if you need it. Come home now and I'll forget how embarrassing it is that you've taken off. And I won't stand for you moping about anymore either. You aren't allowed to be depressed around me."

"I'm not coming home. Ever. And if that pisses you off, then that's a perk for me. I'm depressed, in the event you forgot, because I've lost my husband and child." She would have gone home, but she decided right then and there she was moving to another country, just to be away from her sister.

"And I'm not jealous. I don't even like you."

"Of course you do, Gracie. Everyone loves me. You're so jealous that it's eating you alive. Is that why you took off without a word? To hide? When you get back, you're going to be checked into a hospital and get over this depressing shit that you're doing. It's not making me want to use you as a sitter. You've been down long enough; just get over yourself and come back here."

There wasn't any talking to her, so Gracie closed her phone. She knew that it was going to piss Cora off, but she didn't care anymore. If she died out here, which was what it was looking like would happen, she was sure that Cora would turn it around so that she was the victim in all this.

Gracie looked at the creature in front of her. She had no idea how long he'd been standing there. Gracie supposed in a vague sort of way she'd seen him, but her mind had decided not to. Or something like that. Perhaps her sister was right, she did need to have her head examined.

"Are you real?" The dragon nodded and laid down on the ground in front of her. "I'm not well if you're here. It means that I've either died, which I don't think so—there is too much pain—or I'm off my rocker. Again, not sure how that works since I hurt so fucking much."

The dragon moved closer and she could almost bask in his heat. There hadn't been a lot of warm days lately. His heat felt good, and she put out her hand to touch him.

"Will you eat my hand off if I ask you to come closer? I'm freezing." Her teeth started to chatter now and she shivered. "Come on, warm a girl up, will you?"

He did move closer to her, and wrapped his big wings around her. It was both terrifying and comforting to have so much strength and warmth around her so quickly. Crying softly, she spoke to the dragon. Whether he was real or not, she needed to vent to him.

"I came out on this trip to find myself. And to have some quiet time. My job, it doesn't allow for a lot of that. Mostly it's people screaming at each other about nothing. And then there's my sister. She's a pain in my ass." Almost as if Cora knew she was talking about her, Gracie's phone rang. "My name is Gracie Hobbs, and the woman ringing me to death is Cora Daniels, my older sister. She's a bitch, but she might like to know I've been killed or something. Don't tell her that it was whatever it was…she'll never believe you anyway. I'm pretty sure that was a griffin, but then, I'm not sure of much of anything right now. Other than I'm hurting."

The voices had her stiffening. She wasn't sure who it might have been, but the dragon wrapped around her became a man with arms. Gracie looked up at him. His smile was as warm as his wings had been.

"Am I dead?" He told her that she wasn't going to die. "I feel horrible. I think that thing back there, and I'm not saying what it was, but I think it hurt me."

"His name is Bolrock, and he is very sorry for harming you. My family is here, and we're going to take you to our house." She nodded, sure she was dreaming. "You're not dreaming, Gracie, but you are very ill."

"I hurt too. Don't call my sister or tell my mom." He said that he'd not do that. "Mom is wonderful, but she's having a good time. Unless I die, then you can call them both. But Mom first, she should know that I've died before Cora. Cora is a bitch."

"You said that." Gracie felt herself being helped to lie down. The world started to spin out and she knew was going to be sick. Leaning over, she saw shoes, and a lot of them. Emptying her belly, she knew that the people, the shoe wearers, were going to leave her there after she puked on their pretty shoes.

"I'm sick." Someone said something like no shit, then she heard a very loud slap. "Please, help me. I'm not ready to die. I have things to do. I really thought I was ready for a long time, but not now. I want to see the world. All of it before I want to kick up the dirt, as my mom says."

She felt herself being lifted; strong arms and a warm body held her. Snuggling her nose into his throat, she knew that he was a man that took good care of himself. And the smoothness of his face made her think that he was either very young or had only just shaved. For some reason that made her happy. But her body took that moment to chill again, and she moved closer to him.

"She'll need napkins." Gracie wasn't sure that she heard that right, but nodded. Stopping after two steps, she said she was sick again. That was when it hit her that he wasn't saying napkins but blankets. The person holding her lowered her until she was on the ground again, and she dry heaved three times before he picked her back up. "Mom, what do we do?"

If he said more or if there was even an answer to the question, she didn't hear it. Gracie felt someone touch her on the head and she was simply gone.

Gracie woke up off and on. She knew that things were moving; the view from her prone position was forever changing. Once she woke to see the clouds above her and snowflakes just tumbling down, like they did in those pretty balls. The next time, or perhaps the second or third time, she woke in a room. The ceiling was tin, pressed in pretty patterns that made her think of old houses on that show she watched sometimes. Then once more she woke to find herself in a dark room, with only the sound of a ticking clock and someone snoring.

Her body hurt, though not like it had when she'd made her way back to the path she'd been on. There were places on her that made her think that she had an IV and someone might have tied her arm to the bed. She wasn't sure that she liked that, but she lacked the strength to complain. Closing her eyes, she smelled something wonderful. Like cookies being baked with chocolate.

"Miss?" Gracie opened her eyes and looked at the man standing over her. He was incredibly tall, or she was on the floor again. When he smiled at her, she had a feeling that he knew just what she was thinking. "You're going to be fine now. I need for you to wake just a little more so that I can change out your sheets."

"I'm not dead." He shook his head and moved out of her vision. Another man, this one bigger, took his place. "My goodness, there must be something in the water around here. You guys are monster big, aren't you?"

"Gideon, move back, son. She can't be seeing us with you taking up all the room in front of her. Move back, please." When the man winked at her, then disappeared, she raised her head enough to look. It was difficult...her body felt like she'd been on a bender for about a month, and then someone had the nerve to run over her. "There you are. You're going to be just fine now. My Sally, she knows her herbs and how to fix most ailments."

"Where—?" Gracie felt like her throat had been scrubbed with a brush, and her body hurt so badly that she laid back down and closed her eyes again. "I'm sick."

"You will be weak for a few more days. Not much longer. We thought for sure that we lost you there a couple of times.

You want to sit up a bit?" She said that she thought she'd be better off dying. "Now, don't go talking like that. We need you here. You just go on and rest some more, and when you're awake again, we'll all talk."

"How long?" He told her however long she wanted. "No, I mean, how long have I been here?"

She was sure that she'd heard him wrong, but sleep took her. There wasn't any way she'd been here for nine days. But again, sleep took her. Gracie was glad for it. Maybe, the way she was feeling, she'd wake up dead. No, that wasn't right, just not hurt any more.

Gracie saw her face but had no idea who she was. Nor did she think she was awake. The woman, a beautiful woman that had an air of being kind and rich, stood just in front of a large castle. Moving toward her, slowly so as not to fall on her face, she felt her face heat up when the woman laughed and told her she'd be fine.

"I don't know. I've been pretty sick. I think I might be dead." She assured her that she wasn't. "How do you know? For all you know we could both be dead."

"I am, I'm sad to say." That didn't make any sense, but Gracie nodded. Then, sitting on the ground when asked to, Gracie looked at the castle. "It's beautiful, is it not? My sons and those of Jacob and Sally have done such a wonderful job with it. We never dreamed that they'd be able to accomplish so much."

A man, looking slightly like the one that had winked at her, came to stand beside the woman. They were in love...it looked as if it simply surrounded them in goodness. When the man turned to her, she knew that he was somehow related to the other man. And when he put out his hand to her, she stared at it.

"I have something for you, young Gracie Benson. You will do well, we think, once you are better." She said her name was Hobbs. "Nay, you are a Benson now. We saw you, but knew not what you would bring to our family. The ability to see us is something that we did not see when we had a peek at the future. I'm so happy to make your acquaintance. How are you feeling?"

"I don't know. And I'm sorry, what?" The man laughed and she felt its warmth to her toes. "The woman, she said she was dead. Are you as well?"

"Yes. For a great many years. It's a long story, one full of hope and romance. There is even a little intrigue as well." The woman scolded the man, telling him to get on with it. "Yes, there is little time with us being here. I have a quest for you, Gracie. Would you accept it?"

"Quest? You mean the dead need things done for them? I mean, I've heard that, I guess, but since I've never seen a dead person, or a couple of them, then I'd not really know that, now would I?" They laughed again and she felt a smile tugging at her own lips. "What is this quest you have for me?"

"You are a delight, Gracie. I think that you'll do well with our son." She wasn't sure what that meant, but Gracie figured that she was hallucinating and went with it. "You are paired with Onimia. His counterpart is Gideon. Fine men, the two of them. But what we need for you to do is to tell young Asher, the king of dragons now, to keep his parents close to him in the days ahead. Especially his mother."

"Keep his mother close in the coming days. Yeah, I can do that. Of course." The man nodded at her. "Who are you? I mean, you know my name. So, what is yours?"

"We're the original queen and king of the dragons, Eve and Anthony." Dragons again. Thinking about the last one she'd seen, she asked them about him. "Yes, that was Keion. He's mated to Lelani, a very strong witch that will protect you as well."

"Too many names. All right. I'm to tell Asher, whoever he is, to keep his mom and dad close to him in the coming days. And the rest...well, that's just dressing, isn't it? Dreams are funny like that, I guess." They looked at each other then back at her. "Anything else? I mean, this is partly your dream too, right?"

"Yes, you'll need this." The touch was just a simple hand placed on her head, but when the other hand, that of Eve, joined Anthony's, she knew a real kind of pain. "Go forth, young Gracie, and watch out for your sister. Cora will be causing you a great deal of trouble too."

What else was new, she thought as she felt herself being moved. Almost as soon as the sensation came over her that she was going fast, she stopped. Opening her eyes, she looked around and saw two men, both of whom were sleeping in the chairs next to her. When a hand touched hers, she closed her eyes. Warmth, that's what she thought of, warmth and love.

Chapter 2

Gideon wasn't sure what he was supposed to be looking for, but he searched the grasses where they'd picked up Grace. Onimia had been looking for her clothing or anything else she might have left behind, and had heard a strange noise. They were sent to find its source.

He knew his mate's name but nothing else about her. Which he supposed was all right since she knew nothing about them, not even their names. He looked at Onimia when he said his name.

"Do you hear it?" He did, but he hadn't any idea what it was. "It's a cell phone. I hear them in town too. But that ring...I haven't any idea why that ring is annoying when none of the other sounds I've heard piss me off."

Onimia looked around before smiling at him. Mom could pop out of nowhere, it seemed, and hear them when they didn't want her to. And it didn't matter that Mom wasn't really Onimia's mother, he still respected her enough to not curse in front of her.

They found the noise that had been bothering them. Three

times over the last four hours they'd missed it by inches, he'd bet. Picking it up, he looked at the screen and nearly dropped it when it went off again. Showing it to his brother, he was laughing.

"It's the sister. I'm assuming, anyway." The screen said simply *bitch,* and the sound it was giving off was that of a high-pitched whine, much like a goat did when it was pissed off. "Do you suppose we should answer it? She might have missed her call ins or something. I don't want her to worry."

"I don't know. Even when she was out, Gracie didn't seem to be thrilled with her sister. I mean, the one-sided arguments she was having makes me think that she's right in calling her that." Gideon nodded, but to not be in contact with family bothered him. "What do you think?"

Before he could make the decision, the phone stopped ringing. Gideon had an idea that it would start up again, but put it in his pocket as they picked up the last few items that she'd had. There wasn't much…a few packages of food that something had gotten into, a pretty sweater, and a pair of tennis shoes. The rest of her things they'd gotten a few days after she'd joined their household.

"What do you think of having a mate? I mean, I didn't think we'd be this ready in only a few days, but we did it." Well, Asher had, for them and the rest of them. His mom had even gone over to their new home and had said it would pass. "Do you suppose she'll want to change things up?"

"I haven't any idea. I mean, I don't even understand why she's out here with hardly any protection." Gideon smiled at Onimia's words. "And what if someone had come along when she was alone and hurt her? What would we have done then?"

"If the other women in our family are any indication, I'm

sure that whoever came up on her would have been in for a big surprise. She'd probably knock them around a little before she was left alone." Onimia nodded, his face sort of looking all gloom and doom again. "Aren't you happy about having someone in our life?"

"I'm terrified, if you want to know the truth. I mean, I've never even had sex before, and now we both have a woman that'll want it all the time. I haven't any idea how to satisfy someone. Especially a mate." Gideon told him that it didn't work that way. "How do you know? How many mates have you had? None, that's how many. And not only do we have a mate, but we have one that has been hurt by a griffin. And you know what that means."

"No, not really. Every time I ask someone about it, I get this vague sort of answer. What is it that she's going to gain from this?" The house was getting close to them, so he stopped walking and looked at his other half. "Onimia, what is it that is going to happen to her?"

"He'll be her servant. For all time. For Mark as well, but since he didn't get nearly as sick as she did, then Bolrock will find one of his family to take care of him. And by servant, he'll be something like Roger is to Lelani." Gideon asked why. "I'm not sure. Magic has passed between the two of them, I know that, but Mark got some of it as well. But less so because Bolrock was ready to kill him. I know that he didn't mean to, but that didn't mean anything to us at the time. I suppose we're lucky that she came along when she did. No telling what might have happened."

"I don't understand any of that." Onimia nodded but looked no less grumpy. "What else? I mean, there is more too, right?"

"Yes, but it's hard to know what it might be, this magic

she got. I mean, it could be nothing more than that she can make a few flowers grow to being able to raise the dead. That would be a scary ability to have, don't you think?" Gideon agreed with him. "But she'll figure it out, and then we'll be able to deal with it. Right?"

"Yes."

They went into the house and put the cell phone down on the large table that was in the kitchen. No one was in the warm room, but there were several pots on the stove. He could smell the venison broth even before he picked up the lid for a peek.

Since their mom had come back to them, they'd been eating at the big house nightly and the house had been adjusted for them. The table would have easily held ten people before, but now he'd bet that it would serve twenty or more and still have room left over.

"She's awake." Gideon stared at his mom when she smacked his hand and took the lid from him. "Go on up now and talk to her. She's been resting, falling asleep less and less. Go up and see her."

Gideon went up the stairs behind Onimia. They weren't moving all that fast, neither of them. It was as if they were going to their doom or something. Smiling at the thought, he walked into the big bedroom to find her staggering to the bathroom. They both rushed to her aid.

"I have this." He moved back, but not too far so he'd be able to catch her in case she fell. "I have to pee, is that all right?"

"I suppose it's better than peeing in the bed." Gideon hit Onimia. "What? It is, isn't it? I mean, your mom would have a fit if that happened, and then blame us."

Gracie was staring at them and holding onto the dresser

next to her. Her knuckles were white, she was holding on so tightly. Gideon asked her if they could give her a hand, just to the room.

"I'm weak, not senseless." He wasn't sure why she said that, but when her face reddened, he smiled at her again. "Look, that lady, Miss Sally, she said that you were my mate. I'm not having that. I mean, I have so much going on right now in my head that I can't think beyond going to the bathroom without having my belly churn up again. Just one thing at a time."

"We're both of us your mates." She looked at Onimia, then at him. When he nodded at her, she turned her back on them both. "I'm a dragon too."

Onimia rubbed his chest where Gideon hit him. The man was going to make her bolt, there was no doubt about it. So when she turned and headed for the door, he told his other half to stay there as he followed her out. The stairs gave her some trouble, but after asking if she needed help and being growled at, he stayed back, but well within reach.

"Dragon. And griffins. There was a little person in that room this morning telling me that I had to have her follow me around all the time. I sent her on her way." He asked if she'd gotten her name. "Othello. The name was bigger than she was. And if you think I just shoved her out the window then you're fucking wrong."

"I didn't." She mumbled some more and he watched her. "If you make a right at the end of the staircase, the kitchen is that way. And if you're leaving, which at this point, I don't blame you, you should eat something first."

Gracie stopped at the bottom of the stairs and he moved to stand in front of her. He had no idea what he expected to see on her face, but the tears rolling down her cheeks made

29

his heart hurt. But he wasn't imprudent enough to think that because she was crying, he'd be able to touch her. So he moved closer and asked if he could.

"You've gone through a great deal in the last few days." She nodded and sniffled loudly. "And I would like to tell you, even though you probably don't want to hear it, Bolrock and Mark are very sorry that you were hurt."

"I was only trying to protect the little guy. I never meant for him to be hurt either." Gideon said he knew that too. "I was out hiking. I've been doing it for a few months now. I thought at first it was going to be just an adventure. It still is, but now it's like I'm becoming myself again."

"You were someone else?" When she glared, he smiled. "I don't know you well enough yet to know if this is the real you or the one you're getting away from."

"Neither. I discovered, quite by accident, that I was running from life. Mostly my sister, but that's a can of worms I'm not opening with...where is my cell phone?" He told her it was in the kitchen too. "You didn't answer it, did you? I'm sure that she would have plenty to say to you should you have."

"No. We didn't answer it. But your mom did call a few times as well. And again, we didn't answer it." She headed to the kitchen, her steps getting slower and slower. "I'd like to be able to help you, Gracie. You're not doing yourself any good by wearing yourself out."

"I'm fine." He had a feeling she said that a great deal to people, when it was obvious that she was far from it. "I'm not staying here. I want to finish my walk and enjoy myself."

"Sure. We'll go with you." That stopped her in her tracks, and he bumped into her from behind. And what a fine behind she had too. Gideon held onto her hips, either to hold her steady or himself…he wasn't sure which, but he held himself to her. "You smell of the outdoors. Your hair is as beautiful as anything I've ever seen in nature. And I can smell the magic on you that Bolrock gave you."

"Magic? I don't have any magic." Her voice was low, seductive and husky. He kissed her shoulder where her neck met it. Then he licked a path from there to the back of her ear. "Stop this right now."

He should have been careful. He knew that as he sailed across the room, hitting the wall behind him. And even as his head banged hard on it, Gideon knew that he'd forever love his first taste of her. But when she stormed into the kitchen he sat very still, not hurt, but afraid that if she saw him smiling, she'd come to him and finish him off.

~~~

Gracie didn't know what to expect when she entered the large kitchen. Certainly not a man and woman having a very heated argument. And if she was right, it was over how many flowers, not the milled sort but the growing sort, to put on the cake for a brownie. And Gracie had no idea why she thought this, but she was sure it wasn't brownies like a person ate. They both turned to look at her when a baby cried.

The infant was lying in a crib that had obviously been handmade. Not only did the bed look to be old, but the blanket that covered her did as well. Reaching into the little thing, she picked the little girl up and held her to her breast. Emotions, long since hidden away, tore at her.

"Honey, what is it?" The softly asked question, the way the hand softly touched her arm, nearly took her to her knees. Gracie turned to the couple and looked at them through the blurring tears. "Tell us."

"She was only four months old when she died. They said

it was quick, that they both didn't suffer at all. Cain, he was my husband, he...we had no idea that he had this ticking bomb in his head, and when the aneurysm burst, killing him instantly, he drove the car into the back of a semi." Gracie sat down in the chair, just noticing that both Gideon and Onimia were in the doorway. "We'd only been married for five years. Married young, I guess, but we were so much in love. I was hurt badly, of course."

"I'm so sorry for your loss, child." The baby touched her little fingers to her face, making her heart hurt even more for it. She looked at Sally when she sat beside her. "This is Sally Anne. I'm only just getting to know her too. She has a cousin, Eve Marie, who will be over in a bit. Your husband, did you and he have a good life?"

"Oh yes. He was kind and good to us. And when he died, I wanted to die along with them. There wasn't...it was difficult to want to go on. It still is most of the time, but being out and by myself, I can cry and no one cares." Sally nodded, taking her hand into hers. "My sister, Cora, she blamed me for Beth's death. Said that I should have been driving, that...she never liked Cain. She said that he was reckless and had no talent for what he did. She thinks he was a lazy person when he was far from that."

"Cain Hobbs was your husband?" She nodded at Gideon. "I loved his work. He was one of the best photojournalists I've ever had the pleasure of meeting. His death put a huge hole in the journalist world. I'm so sorry for your loss."

"You met him? When was that?" He told her. "Yes, that was his best showing. And it was also the last time he was at an event where the public knew he was there. He never cared for the limelight. After that, he just stayed in the shadows and watched people, even taking their pictures as they looked at his. We'd have so much fun after the show, looking at the faces of people as they took in his work."

"He was a great.... Why would your sister call him reckless?"

Gracie smiled sadly as she told Onimia Cora's reason's for disliking her husband. "She thought that no one could make a good living by selling pictures of animals and underdeveloped countries. No matter how many times I told her that he was paid well and left me well off, she never believed me. Not that I had to justify myself to her, but that is one of the reasons that she thinks I'm a fool." Gracie gave the baby to Sally when she reached for her grandma. "I should be going. I mean, this has been nice, I guess, resting up here, but I need to get going again."

"Don't go. Not yet." She asked Onimia why not. "Well, for one thing, you're still weak. And the second reason is, I'd very much like to get to know you. And you us."

"I don't have it in me to love another person, Onimia. I loved once, and that is it for me." He nodded, but didn't agree or disagree with her really. "You should really try and find someone that isn't damaged."

"We're all damaged in some way." She looked at Jacob. "And when you've been around for as long as we have, you get your heart bruised up more than most. The king and queen dying and leaving us—"

"She was in my dream." Gracie felt foolish when she cut Jacob off. "I'm sorry. You must think I'm an idiot. But I had the most vivid dream about a king and queen. They told me that they were the dragon king and queen. That Asher, whoever he is, he was the current one and that I was to give him a message."

"That's our oldest son." She frowned. "What was the

message? I mean, if you can tell us."

"They told me about you. I mean the two of you." She pointed at Gideon and Onimia. "I'm to tell Asher to keep his parents close, especially his mom. And that my sister was going to be causing me trouble. But that's nothing new."

"Did they say why?" She told Sally that they hadn't. "What else? Anything that we should know about them?"

"Yes. They said that I could see them because of my being hurt, and then the guy, Anthony, he touched his hand to my head and said that I'd need this." Gracie thought about the conversation a little harder. "They said that they knew I'd be coming. But that's not possible. I didn't even know that you were here. But they said that while they knew that I'd be coming here, they didn't know what I'd be bringing. And Anthony, he called me delightful. No one has ever called me that before."

No one moved. She didn't know what to think…the way they were staring at her made her realize that she'd said something wrong. But the longer they stared, the more upset she became. Standing up, she was ready to get out of there before they got pissy when her cellphone rang. She picked it up and answered before thinking that this was not the time to talk to Cora.

"Where the hell have you been? I have been trying to contact you for two fucking weeks, Gracie. What a thing to do to me. I wanted to tell you this great news, and you didn't even have the gumption to answer the phone. Now I don't know whether you deserve to know or not." Gracie wanted to hang up on Cora, but before she could make good on her thought, Gideon took the phone from her and put it on speaker. "Gracie, stop acting like an immature brat and ask me what my good news is. Damn it, it's always about you, isn't it?"

"I'm fine, thanks for asking." Cora huffed and told her that her news was too important for her to think of her. "Of course it is. It's always too important when it's about you, isn't it? What news do you have? Not that I care."

"I'm going to have another baby. And thank you so fucking much for taking the joy out of it for me. You are the most selfish person I know, Gracie. You always have been." Cora made a sniffling sound, like she was really hurt. But Gracie knew it was all a ploy to make her apologize. But no more. "You've been like this since that accident. People die all the time, Gracie, get over it and move on. He wasn't that much of a husband anyway or he'd have taken better care of—"

"I told you before, you are not to speak to me about my husband." Cora huffed at her. "I'm hanging up now, Cora. I'm happy for you, but I don't want to talk to you right now."

"You most certainly will not hang up on me. I have good news, damn it, and you're going to be happy for me." Gracie looked at Onimia when he growled. "What are you doing now? Hanging out with dogs? Gracie, you are never going to amount to anything if you don't get your life on track as I have. I have a good husband who has a good job, who makes sure we have a good home and our children are safe. What do you have? Nothing, and you never will so long as you don't take responsibility for your actions. As soon as you get home, I'm going to expect some major changes in you. No more acting like you've lost your best friend. And you will not avoid me. I need you to get back here, because Mother isn't answering her phone. It will do you some good to be normal again. I certainly can't stand you this way."

The conversation was being heard by them all. More

35

people had shown up, and Gracie wanted to cry. It was bad enough that Cora had this opinion about her and her life, but to have others hear it too was painfully embarrassing. Before she could cut her off, however, Gideon spoke.

"Who the hell do you think you are, talking to her that way? Can't you get your head out of your ass for ten seconds and find out why she didn't answer her phone? Or even to ask if she's getting along all right?" Cora asked who he was. "My name is Gideon Benson, and I'm in love with your sister. You are a rude woman, and you should be ashamed of yourself."

"In love? With my sister?" The laughter made her pissed off. Again. "She's not one to fall in love with, Gideon. Hasn't she told you? My goodness, she has nothing now. Less than nothing. All she had she sold off or gave away when she got it in her head to run off like she did. Just because I told her that she was better off as a widow than married to a man who used his camera to take pictures instead of holding down a real job, like the rest of the world does. What sort of living is that, I ask you? She could have been married to a doctor or an attorney. Or an accountant, like I am. But no, she had to marry an artist. Tell me where she is and I'll come there and tell you all about my lovely baby sister. She's no more a prize than the trash I have taken out to the bin daily."

"Whatever you have to say, it means nothing to me." Cora laughed again. "And pray, what do you find so funny about that?"

"You sound just like Cain. 'Oh, I don't care that she's just working as a security guard. I'm in love with her.' See what that got him? Dead. And instead of just killing himself off, he took their daughter with him. Selfish bastard. But all's well that ends well if you ask me. All this happened to her because my dear sister wanted to go on a vacation that neither of them could afford." With shaking hands, Gracie wrote down how much money was in her accounts. And what she owned. As Cora went on about what she had or didn't have in this case, she wanted her to know that she had plenty. "Did she tell you about our mother? When our father died, with the exception of her house she sold off everything she had, which in my estimations couldn't have been that much, and took a trip. Leaving me here not just without a sitter, but without someone to keep an eye on my home when we take trips as a family. Selfish...my entire family is selfish and jealous of everything I have."

"You ever think it might be you that's the selfish one? All I've heard from you is that someone did this to you. Or that they left you without. What about Gracie? What do you think she lost in that accident?" Cora said she was better off. "How could you say that?"

"She's my sister and I can say those things to her. And don't think that just because you claim to be in love with her, you're going to make me stop. It's how I do things, honesty all the way. Gracie needs to have her head checked out and get her ass back here. With Mother gone off on her little getaway, I could use her to sit for me if she's not going to work." Gideon took her hand in his and she held it. Onimia stood behind her, his hands on her shoulders. "Tell me where she is. I'm coming to straighten her out."

She didn't think he was going to continue talking to Cora, but not only did he tell her his address, but asked if she wanted him to send someone to get her. That made her laugh, and Cora told him that she had a car that could take her wherever she wanted.

"I mean a plane. I can have one there for you in a few hours." Cora didn't say anything then, and Gracie had to smile. It was a good bluff, but she'd not believe it even if there was a jet sitting on the tarmac fueled up and ready to go for her. "Tell me when you're ready, Cora, and I can have one there for you in a couple of hours."

"Very funny. And what is it you do for a living? Don't tell me. You're a painter. You paint houses for a living, but you have big plans for when someone gives you a break. I got news for you, buster, I'm not now nor will I ever give you a dime just because you're thinking yourself in love with Gracie." Gideon asked her if Cain had ever borrowed money. "No, he knew better. And Gracie has always hated me because I have so much more than she'll ever have. You know why? Because she's never going to amount to anything. She's far too lazy and unwise to see that."

Gideon closed the connection. And then, with extreme care, he laid the phone on the table. When he looked at Gracie she saw it, the anger that looked to be boiling over close to the surface. And for whatever reason, she wasn't afraid of him. He was controlled, that was all she could think about...his anger was controlled.

"Do you have insurance on this thing?" She shook her head. "Not that it matters, but I'm going to destroy it. Not your sister, though. She needs to have her ass kicked, but I don't want her calling you again. Not if all she is going to do is spew shit like that at you."

"I'll do it." Gideon handed the phone to Onimia and he laid it in the sink. When he shifted, his body becoming a beautiful but deadly looking dragon, she watched as he blew a short burst of flames over the phone, destroying it for all time.

Gracie laughed. It was that or just break down and cry. Standing up, she made her way out of the house and onto the porch that wrapped around it. Sitting in the swing that was there, she cried. Simply sobbed when she thought of what these people might think of her now.

Chapter 3

Essie heard about the conversation between Cora and Gideon. Every time she thought of the sister, Essie wanted to go and murder her in her sleep. It wouldn't solve anything, but she'd feel good about it, she thought. And apparently, Cora was coming here. Essie saw Lindsey coming out of her house just as Sally and Jacob were coming from the direction of the castle.

Since talking to Gracie, they'd had faeries with them always. Right now, Essie could see at least a dozen of them flying around them, and she had to smile. Jacob wasn't too thrilled about having them around when he wanted to court his mate...his words, not hers. Still, until they knew what was going to happen, it was better to take all precautions.

Lindsey joined her, their babies bundled up in blankets and coats. It was cold out, but they needed the sunshine too. They both tried to bring them out for a little bit every day. And the babies seemed to enjoy it. Sitting on one of the blankets made for just this sort of outings, the two hugged and started talking.

"I was just talking to Gideon. He said that Cora is coming in the morning. I cannot wait to meet this bitch." Essie turned to see Gracie coming around the side of the house, both her mates hot on her tail. "She's having a hard time of it. I mean, Onimia said that they were trying hard to give her space, but she's not wanting them anywhere near her. I feel for all three of them."

"She's hurting still. I'm not sure that it's the loss of her husband and child, or the way her sister seems to think she's stupid and needs her head examined. Literally." Essie thanked Elbert for the tea and scones and took a blueberry one before Lindsey did. "I've done some research on Cora. Well, all of them, really. It seems that Miss Cora isn't as well off as she has led everyone to believe. And having her sister under her thumb might be more of a ploy to get her to come live with them, for some extra income, rather than just needing a free sitter."

"How bad is it?" Essie told her. "That's not horrific, is it? I mean, I know some people that have twice that much in credit card debt. Forty grand, that's not a figure that is too out of reach."

"It is if you're constantly spending more than you have coming in. And the private school where the kids are going is wanting their payments too. They owe from this term and the last two. Then there is the company credit card. I'm still trying to figure that one out. Why do you suppose she keeps harping on Gracie about her life if hers is ten times worse?" Lindsey said she didn't know and wondered about that as well. "When she gets here, I don't think things are going to go well for her. Cora has been picking at Gracie for far too long, and she needs to crack. And I'm sure it's going to be her head, not Gracie's."

"I looked up about the accident. There wasn't anything anyone could have done to save him. The aneurysm wasn't seen by the slew of tests he had done the week before. He was the picture of health, they told them, and he was headed for this long vacation before he started on a new assignment. And the baby.... I can't imagine losing a child like that." Essie nodded. "But I've noticed too that she loves to hold our babies. And cuddles with them a great deal. Perhaps she just needs one of her own. If they can ever get together."

"I have an idea about that. It's not bad, but perhaps if we can get them closed up someplace, like a cave or something, we can expedite things along for them. I was going to ask Sally about it. I cannot believe how easily she slipped right back into her role as parent to these boys of hers." They both laughed. "I had no idea that Lelani knew her, did you?"

"Not in the capacity that she did, no. I mean, I knew of them, the Bensons, but never had all that much to do with them." Essie picked up Sally Anne when she fussed and looked around as Lindsey continued. "I'm worried."

"About what? I mean, if you're worried, then the rest of us should be as well, I'm thinking." Lindsey didn't laugh as she hoped that she would. "What is it? Something is coming, isn't it?"

"Yes. Two days ago, or three, I can't remember, I saw some signs of a hunter in the woods. I called some people in to have a look, and they've found two groups of people just beyond the border of this land that are getting ready for something. To me, what they're carrying indicates that they're going after dragons. Iron, it would be what they'd need if we weren't all immune to it. But it can still kill those that aren't here yet." Essie hadn't thought of that, that the other dragons coming wouldn't be safe until they were here. "If there are two out

43

there, I'm thinking that there will more than likely be more coming to us. And I don't know what to do to keep them safe. I think we need a family meeting."

"Good idea. I'll have a look around too, and perhaps we can get the other witches and earthling creatures to keep an eye out too. Not that we don't anyway, but since we're going to Sally and Jacob's tonight, we could talk it over then." Essie thought of the family dinners they'd been having and smiled. "I think that I might have to go on a diet if we eat there every night for the rest of our days. Sally is making up for lost time, I think."

Essie looked around and thought of all the people and other beings here. There was so much riding on them keeping everyone safe. And they were, but not until they got here.

She nearly burst out laughing when Gracie sat down with them. The look on her face was murderous, and Essie would bet anything that Gideon and Onimia had gotten an earful from her. She almost felt sorry for them. Almost, but she knew that it would work out for the three of them.

"They're driving me crazy. All I wanted to do was take a long walk, alone, and they were right there with me. And if they weren't, they were in my head. I'm not used to having people around all the time." She picked up Eve Marie and kissed her chubby cheek before continuing. "Also, I don't know if you guys know this or not, but I can talk to the dead."

No one said anything. Essie knew that she'd been in contact with the former queen; not only did she smell of her magic, but she told them that she'd been given something by the king. She wondered, as Asher had, what sort of magic she'd been given. But this was well beyond her contacting them for information, this was.... Well, fucking messed up. Essie wasn't sure how to proceed, but Lindsey, in her usual fashion, just came right out with her questions.

"You talk to them or you have a conversation with them?" Gracie asked her what the difference was. "You're off your noodle in the first one, or you're special in the second. Though talking to a dead person…I have no idea what that would do for us, but it's something we can work with."

"I have conversations with them. And you know what? I think I don't like you. You're very brash, aren't you?" She said it with a smile, as if she'd been kidding, but Essie wasn't so sure. Gracie was a hard one to nail down. "And it is useful. Something I should have mentioned too was that I can talk to all dead things. Including the dragons and a couple of faeries that were killed by something."

"Holy fuck." Lindsey looked at her with the strangest look on her face. "I heard that three faeries and a small dragon were killed just the other day, before they got here. The dragon was mistaken for a dragonfly, thanks to the faeries that lost their lives with him."

"Right, it was them. They said that the men that killed them hadn't any idea what they were, other than horseflies, and that their magic went to the queen." The baby in Gracie's arms started to fuss, and Lindsey handed her a bottle as she continued. "Also, I'm to tell Asher—why him, I have no idea—but to tell him that the time is coming where he is going to have to finish up the castle completely and take a stand. I don't know what that means. I've never seen the castle. Mutt and Jeff, my counterparts, have been hanging around too much for me to do anything on my own."

"Mutt and Jeff? You know, I don't care." Essie laughed. "You're going to have to give into them sooner or later. I mean, not sexually, though that is beyond words fantastic, but to give them a little help. They're hurting."

"I can't. Don't you see? I just...I love your babies. They're what makes me want to stick around. And the rest of you guys, you're so sweet and nice. Most of the time, anyway." Her pointed look at Lindsey had them both laughing. "But I can't have another child. I can't...I was hurt badly in the accident, and there isn't anything left in me to...They want children, I know that, but I can't give them any. Ever."

"I'm so sorry." Gracie burped the baby then handed her to Lindsey. When she stood up, so did Essie. "Don't leave. Please. If you do, then...I don't know what would happen to them should you leave. But having you in their lives is going to be more than enough for them. I promise you this. And if it's not, then I'll help you pack. I swear it."

"They...I don't know. Cora is coming tomorrow; did you know that?" They said that they did. Gracie started pacing the snow-covered ground in hard stomps. "She's not a nice person. Her kids are privileged brats, and her husband is a know-it-all jerk. Not that they're not suited for each other, but they belittle anyone they're around."

"I've talked to your mom." That stopped her from pacing. And when she turned to look at her, Essie could see the love for her mom. "She's coming here sometime today. I've sent a plane for her. I didn't invite her, not really, but when she found out that Cora was coming, she said it was about time she had a long talk with her daughter. And she's glad to be able to see you too."

"I talked to her last night. She never mentioned she was coming." Essie told her that she'd spoken to her earlier that morning. "Why would you do that? I mean, I thank you for it, but why would you invite another stranger to your place?"

"It's your place here too, and I wanted you to be happy. It wasn't my idea anyway, as I said. But so you know, Gideon gave me the number from your phone, and asked me if I could contact her, just to let her know you were all right."

Gracie stood there for several minutes. None of them spoke, but Essie could almost touch Gracie's emotions, they were so strong. When she finally turned to them, she had tears on her cheeks and she looked beaten. Essie moved forward to hug her, but she took a step back. Pain shot through her like a knife, but before she could let the hurt take her fully — being turned away did that to her — she looked at Gracie's face.

"Don't move." Essie nodded and looked down at her daughter, who had fallen asleep. "You have a person beside you that has...I'm not sure what they have, but they want me to tell you something."

"All right. Can you tell me who it is?" Gracie nodded but didn't say anything. "Do I want to know who it is?"

"She's a witch. And from the way she's dressed, I'd say she's been long gone." Lindsey asked her for her name as well. "She doesn't remember it, but she said to tell you that she cooked in the castle when she was alive. The first one."

"All right. What is it she needs from me?" Gracie nodded, but Essie thought it was that she was answering the witch and not her. Waiting was making her crazy, but she thought that it was more than just the two of them talking. There had to be something going on too.

"She said to tell you that there is a building closer to the waterline that has a book in it that should be put with the others. She said that it is her book of spells, and she worries that one of the men coming will find it. It's a laymen's book. Do you know what that means?" Essie told her that she didn't, but she knew someone that might. "All right. She said that it is leather bound and spelled. It took me a moment to figure out what that meant. But she said only the blood of the future queen can open it."

"Me?" Gracie shook her head. "Then I don't understand. Who other than me is the queen?"

"She said a child of your blood."

~~~

Gideon looked over the house again. It had been only a few hours since he'd asked Asher to enlarge the kitchen. It was beautiful, and as big as any he'd ever been in. Including his mom's. As he made his way around the large work island, he ran his hands over the wooden surface, marveling at the smoothness of it. Gracie coming in the back door had him turning to her.

"It's beautiful." He was so glad that she liked it that he wanted to hug her. But after talking to Essie a few minutes ago, he was holding off. She needed more space than they were giving her. "I can cook, can you?"

"Yes. Not a lot of things off the cuff, but I can cook well with instructions." She nodded and touched the large wooden structure. "Asher can do all sorts of things with his magic. I can as well. Like if I were to touch you.... May I?"

Gracie looked hesitant, but he was all right with that too. When she finally nodded, Gideon touched his finger to her skin and smiled when her breath caught.

"That was fantastic." He'd given her a little of himself too when he'd warmed her up. He could also cool her off in the summer should she need it. "It's as if you've dipped me in a hot tub. I love that. What else can you do?"

"You can as well, should you want, but we can dress ourselves with a thought. And while I can't shift into a dragon like Onimia can, I can breathe fire when I want." He blew a little flame to his palm and held it for her. "Put out your hand. If you feel heat I'll stop, but I'd like to see if you can hold onto it too."

She put out her hand without any kind of reluctance this time. He transferred the flame to her hand and watched her face when it lit up. Gideon watched her carefully so that she didn't hurt herself. And when Gracie transferred the flame to her other hand, he knew she was going to be all right with it.

"Can I make it larger? I mean, like enough to burn a fire in a pit?" He showed her how to hold it just so and to blow over it. Not only did it get bigger, but hotter too. "This is fantastic. I can see all kinds of uses for something like this."

"It's just as easy to put out too. All you have to do is close your hand around it." She did so and smiled at him. Gideon felt the power of it like she's stroked him across the heart. When Onimia joined them in the kitchen, she showed him what she could do.

Gideon wondered if she had any idea that she'd just created flame on her own. And was sure that Onimia understood. As she played with it, showing him how she could do different things with it, the dragon spoke to him.

I'm in love with her. He told him he was as well. *She's so delightful and funny. Sad too, but knowing why helps somewhat. But I do want to help her.*

As do I. I'm assuming that you spoke to Essie as well. He told her he had. *Good. We'll have to be slow with her, just so she knows we're not going to hurt her.*

She's an immortal. I don't think we should tell her that either. Not yet, at any rate. Gideon agreed with him. *Also, she is thinking about cooking us dinner, and she's not sure how anyone would feel about that.*

What do you mean? Onimia told him about how they'd been going to his parents' house every night. *I'm sure that they won't care if we miss tonight. Besides, making her happy and secure*

49

tonight might make tomorrow better for her.

Showing her the rest of the house was a joy. Gracie loved what the living room looked like, how they'd used natural woods for the floor and the walls rather than the fabricated things. She touched her fingers to everything. It was very telling, to him, telling him what she cared for and what she loved. There was little that she didn't like, but he was going to have Asher help him out with the windows at the back of the house. They were too small. Gracie wanted to be able to see the entire woods, not just the small versions of it that they had now.

I can do that. While I'm talking to you, I just now got a call from the pilot, and her mom will be landing in about an hour. You want to go and meet her? Gideon told Asher that he did. *Good. Also, before I forget to tell you, Cora is bitching about her accommodations. I hope Gracie doesn't mind, but I had them put up in the hotel in town. Apparently her sister did some kind of search on it and it's just not up to her standards. She isn't making me like her very much.*

I don't think I'd sweat it, Asher. I don't think any of us are going to like her. Asher laughed. *I'm going to talk to Gracie about going into town, then I'll contact you. We've been giving her some space, as Essie told us, and playing with our magic. She can make flame. I don't know why I thought that we had to be true mates to share magic, but she can.*

Good. Perhaps she'll do us all a favor and burn the sister to a crisp and we'll be done with it. Asher said he was joking, but Gideon could tell that he was stressed out about this visit. *This has to be done, I know that, but it makes me a little on edge to have someone like that around here. She won't be able to come here either, if she isn't nicer. Gracie is family now, and we'll have to keep her safe from her.*

50

I think this is long in coming too, so I'm not too worried about her. Asher told him that if he wasn't then he wouldn't be either. *I'll get back to you soon.*

She was so excited to know that her mom was coming soon that he nearly forgot to show her the enlarged windows. When she stood staring out of them for several minutes, he went to stand with her. That was when he saw him.

"Who is that?" Gracie just turned and looked at him. "I don't know who that is or how he ended up here, but I don't want you going out there until we check him out."

"You really don't know him?" He shook his head and looked at Onimia when he joined them at the window. "Onimia, do you know him? I mean, you don't recognize him at all?"

"No. Should I?" Gracie nodded at him and smiled. "Why is it I get the feeling that you not only know who that is, but what he wants?"

"I've talked to him before. I told you about it." She laughed, sounding so strange surrounding the circumstances of what was going on. "I can't believe that you'd not know your own father."

"My father is dead." Onimia looked at Gracie, and then Gideon saw the exact moment when he understood what she was telling them. "My father is out there. He's come to…I can see him."

"Yes, but you should know that they'll never come to be with us like Sally and Jacob. They died quietly in their sleep. The king and queen, your parents, died violently, and that will prevent them from coming whole. Something about revenge and not reaping their deaths upon others. I don't know why I should know that, but there is a lot of information in my head about dealing with the dead. I'm not going to freak out

51

about it so long as you two don't. Okay?" Gideon had heard that before. He didn't remember in what context, but he did remember someone saying that. "Would you like to go see what he wants?"

"I don't know, to be honest. It's…I want to talk to him, but he's a stranger to me." Gracie moved to the door and Gideon stood with his other half. "I wouldn't even know what to say to him."

"True. But this might be your only chance. Do you think he has any idea what to say to you?" Onimia looked at him, tears of a dragon sliding down his cheeks. "At least go out and tell him hello. There won't be any harm in that."

"No. No, there won't be." As they moved to join Gracie, Gideon noticed that she was talking to the king. "She's very comfortable with this. I've been wondering if her dead husband would be around."

That stopped him in his tracks and he stood there for several seconds. Could he? Would he come to talk to their mate? And if so, would her child come as well? Suddenly he was terrified of this new magic that was given to them. He didn't even know who to ask about it.

He decided on Caroline. Or Gobi. He wasn't sure they'd know, but he'd talk to them. And perhaps Bolrock. Gideon wasn't sure that he could talk to the big beast, but he thought that it wouldn't hurt to try. He'd been the one to share his magic with her…the least he could do was tell them a bit about it. They were making some headway in being her mates; though he had a feeling a deceased husband and child coming back would be terrible for all of them.

Chapter 4

Cora wasn't happy. There were better accommodations in this town and she knew it. But she'd not complain. It wasn't in her to do so to a stranger who was only trying to help her regain control over her family. They were an embarrassment. And it was well past time that she did something about them.

"William, the children have been fussy all afternoon. Why don't you take them to some little park and let them burn off some energy? Just don't allow them to get dirty. I don't want to have to change them again." Not to mention, she needed a break from every one of them. "An hour and no longer, William. We don't want them to get any germs."

The nanny hadn't been able to come with them at the last minute, giving Cora no choice but to fire the woman. It wasn't her problem that there had been an accident and her mother needed her. That's what she paid her for, to be there for her when she required help. No one, it seemed to her, took responsibility for their actions any longer.

Her sister was here in this godforsaken town. There wasn't even a dry cleaner here, not to mention a mall. Cora's plan had been to do a little Christmas shopping while here, perhaps find something that no one else would ever think to have. She'd be lucky now if she didn't leave here with some sort of disease or something. Cora looked around the room and decided that she was going to spruce it up a bit when talking about it to her friends. Not a lie, but just a little fib. They'd never believe her anyway if she told them what the room actually looked like.

When William took the kids out of the room, she laid down on the bed. It wasn't up to her usual standards either, but she was exhausted and this pregnancy wasn't giving her any kind of relief. The doctor had said something about her not having any more when she'd had Mike, but she'd proven her wrong. As she lay there, closing her eyes against the sunlight, she thought of her sister and mother.

Cora had never liked Cain. And the reasons why were something that she'd take her to her grave. He has spurned her...not once, but three times. And she had hated him for that. Cora was used to getting everything she wanted when she got out of her family home, and Cain wouldn't have her.

"I'm married to your sister. Have you no shame?" She said that she didn't, not really. "Well, it's not going to happen, Cora. I don't want to mess up the best thing that has ever happened to me by having an affair with you, with anyone, for that matter, but especially never you. You're not a very nice person."

"You're not either, but that's beside the point. No one would have to know, Cain. Just a little fling between the two of us." He said that he would know. "So? Stop being such a shit and fuck me, Cain. You know that you want to. I'm better looking than Gracie, and I have what it takes to make a man come twice in one night."

"You're not better looking than my Gracie. Plus, she's the most loving and wonderfully trustworthy person I have ever met. And I love her. As far as your sexual goals in bed, Gracie gives me more than I could ever think you'd be able to. Should I ever think about having sex with you." Cora had been so pissed that she slapped him. "I'll allow you that one time, but you ever draw back to slap me again and I will break your arm."

She remembered being tempted. To wipe that smirk off his face with her hand again would have given her great satisfaction. But she was also afraid of him in that moment. He looked at her with a smile, but it never reached his eyes. She'd had a feeling then, and still did, that had she hit him, even to graze her fingers over his cheek, he would have done just what he said he would and snap her arm as if it was nothing more than a twig. It was then that she decided that she was going to bad mouth him every chance she got. And him dying like he did, it gave her the perfect reason to tell her sister what a loser she'd married.

Cora must have fallen asleep despite the mattress, and woke when the phone rang. Answering it, annoyed that she was being bothered, she didn't care who it was, she was going to give them a piece of her mind. Then the person on the other end laughed.

"Mother? What? How did you get this number?" Mother laughed again, telling her it wasn't that hard if you knew the right people. "You don't know anyone that important. What is it you need now? If it's money, I'm not going to bail you out because you left me without a sitter. What do you do all day that requires you to think you needed to get away? Nothing. I demand that you stop this foolishness and get back to your home immediately. You're too old for traveling around like a younger person anyway. I will take your car from you if you force me to."

"My goodness, how you do go on about things that don't concern you. Cora, I don't know if you remember this or not, but I'm a good deal older than you, and have pictures that would embarrass you at that fine country club you go to." Mother spoke to someone else about lunch and Cora sat up on the bed. "I didn't call to argue with you. Though, I'm pretty sure that's all you do when you talk to someone. But I'm calling to ask you what time you're coming for dinner tonight. There are plans that have to be made, and without—"

"Dinner? With you? Mother, if you called me here, you know very well that I'm not at home. And I don't eat the kind of foods that you cook. I've told you that. Why you feel that deep frying everything and then covering it in that slop you call gravy is healthy is beyond me. But I am happy to know that when I get back home, you'll be there to help us with the children. You have no idea what sort of lengths I've had to go to in order to get—"

"I'm not home. And I'm not sitting your children any longer. I told you that before I left for my cruise. I'm done doing for others. It's time I did things for me. And I plan on doing a lot of things you will disapprove of. I'm going to live my life the way I want to, on my terms." Cora rolled her eyes. "I'm at Gracie's house. I arrived last night."

"What do you mean, Gracie's house? And don't think we won't talk about what you've said about babysitting my children. They're your grandchildren, and it's your obligation to watch them for me. Besides, I'm sure you will want to make sure that I'm well rested. William and I are going to have another child." She smiled at that. Another baby to hold and love. When she didn't get the congratulations that she wanted, she snapped at her mother again. "Mother, what are you talking about, being at Gracie's?"

"Just what I said. And I know about the baby. Is it William's?" Cora felt her heart stop. Just simply stop beating. "Anyway, dinner will be served at six and a car will be around to pick you up at four-thirty. It's pretty far out from town. Such a lovely home. But we'll be eating with her new husbands' family. I started to tell you to be on your best behavior, but we both know that's not going to be happening."

"Husband? What the hell are you talking about?" Her mother laughed again. "Mother, I do not appreciate being the butt of whatever joke you're pulling on me. I demand that you tell me where you are and what you're doing lying to me. I have been with the children all day, and I have a headache. Where are you really? You're going to have to make this up to me by watching the children all night now. I will not tolerate you treating me this way. You and Gracie are going to have to learn your place."

"Our place? You really are an uppity bitch, aren't you? And I've never lied to you, Cora. I think that's why you dislike me so much. I simply don't care for your bullshit, nor do I believe anything that spews from your over puffed lips. As I said to you before, I know you better than anyone and have the pictures to prove it. And just a heads up, your sister isn't going to be such a pushover either any more. You try that shit you did before on her, and I'm sure that she'll break your arm." It was too soon after the memories to think it was just a coincidence. "Have a lovely afternoon, Cora. I'll see you this evening. Oh, and don't even think about running. The plane you came in on isn't for your own personal use."

Putting the phone back in the cradle, Cora sat there for several minutes. Her mind, it seemed, had just frozen up as well, because there wasn't a single thought in her head that she could recall. Standing up, she held onto the post of the bed and rubbed her hand over the small bump that she had only recently developed. Is it William's? her mother had asked.

Her mother knew. That was all she could think about now that she was moving around again. Cora packed her clothing up, thinking to get out of town now, but then unpacked it again when she thought about what she was doing. Running. She was running. And Cora never ran from problems. She was more of a bully people into believing things the way she wanted them to person.

She wasn't a bitch, no matter how many times she'd been told she was. Cora thought of herself as a modern thinking woman. One that was strong enough to hold her own. Have thoughts that were her own as well. If that made her a bitch, then so be it. She was a better woman than most of her friends because she knew what she wanted and went after it.

Cora would take her family to this person's house, get to the bottom of this charade that Gracie was pulling, and expose her for what she was. A lazy woman who had nothing at all to show for her life on this earth. And her husband hadn't been any better. She was glad that he'd died. It was a shame about the baby, but it wouldn't have been any different than her parents. Lazy as the day was long.

When the limo pulled up, they were ready to go. William had wanted to stay home with the kids when he found out that her mother was going to be there, but she told him this was a show of force.

"Cora, I don't think this is the sort of dinner that the boys will enjoy. I know that I don't think I will. Let me stay here with them, you meet with your sister and mom, and then be on your way. And when you return, I think we need to sit

58

down and talk, you and me." She told him they were going and that was the end of it. "We'll eat then get out of there. I'm not even sure why you want to go in the first place."

"Because Gracie needs to be exposed for the person she is. Did I tell you that she's saying that she's married again?" William nodded. "She's a senseless twit. Doesn't she realize that I can and will search out records to prove that she's lying? I have to do this to her. If for no other reason than for her to see things my way and stop being an embarrassment to us all. Mother too. My God, William, she actually told me that she wasn't sitting for the kids any more. What sort of grandmother does that to her only grandchildren?"

Yes, this was a smart move. To put them in their places and move on. Once they were all home again, then she'd be the smart one. She might even have them both declared unfit to handle money and be in charge of it herself. That way, there wouldn't be any more trips that inconvenienced her. Not that they had much anyway.

~~~

"We have something for you." Gracie turned and looked at Gideon. Onimia was right beside him. "You know that your mom told your sister that you were married to us, correct?"

"Yes. I guess that Ariannona thought it would be a better move to make my sister leave us alone. I don't think it'll work, just so you know. Cora is the type of person that sees only her way and fuck the rest. Even if she has no proof whatsoever." Gideon nodded and they both came further into the room with her. "Here is the book that I rescued for the witch. She said to have Asher put it with the rest of them, in a safe place."

He took the book and put it on the table. She didn't tell them that she'd been able to see what was inside the book. Not opened it, but to see the words written in it. She barely

59

understood most of it, but she had promised someone that she'd get it and so she had. The rest, she supposed, was up to Asher.

"Back to what we got you." He put out his closed hand and she stared at it without speaking. "We went to the caves and found one that we thought would suit you. And there are other pieces that go with it. We'd not seen it until today. But then, if you saw where these things were, you'd understand completely. It's sort of a mess in there."

She was afraid to reach out to take it. Gracie knew it was going to be something that she wasn't going to like. The others, the other women, they had huge rings on their fingers. Diamonds and rubies that suited them. But for her.... Well, she wasn't sure what she would want, but big wasn't it.

She turned in her seat so that she was facing them and tried to think what to tell them. The beginning, she supposed, was as good a start as any. Taking a long breath in, she let it out slowly as she began.

"When I met Cain, he was a struggling artist. Well known, I guess, but struggling all the same. I had a good job—it paid our bills—and when he asked me to marry him, there wasn't any way for me to turn him down. I loved him with all that I was." Onimia took her hand in his and kissed the back of it while she continued. "We didn't have a great deal, not at first, but as the pictures he was taking started to gain popularity, the money started coming in more. Then we got pregnant with Beth."

"I read that the car seat that she was in was at fault for her death." Gracie nodded at Gideon. "And that they settled out of court with you."

"I didn't know that was going on. My attorney, a friend of my dad's, he went to bat for me. And since Cain had had

60

a physical the week before and they hadn't found anything, and I guess they should have, he sued the doctor as well as the hospital. I'm very wealthy. But broken." The ring was put on the table in front of her and she laughed. "I don't know why, but I thought you'd go for large. This is…I finally took Cain's ring off this morning. I'm not saying that I'm in love with the two of you, but after a talk with my mom, I want to try and make things work. But you have to know that physically, I can't have children. Not ever."

"So long as we have you, we don't care." She asked Onimia if he was sure about that. "Yes, very sure. You're our life, both mine and Gideon's, and children will come to us. Perhaps not of our bodies, but we'll have as many as you wish."

She still hadn't picked up the ring. Gracie fingered it, moving it around so that she could see the band and the stone, and she looked at them when Gideon asked if they could put it on her. Gracie asked them why they'd picked this stone.

"Gobi told us what it meant and what it was when we took it to her this morning. Caroline said she'd never seen the queen wear it, so it must have been sitting there, waiting for one of us to find." Gideon picked it up and showed her the inscription. He smiled at her as he continued. "This wasn't in the band when we found it. It appeared when we figured out what it was. It was meant for us to give it to you, Gracie."

"'To our darling love, Gracie. Ours forever, G & O.'" She held the ring in her hand as Onimia continued. "This stone, sometimes called the stone of the heavens, aids in the pursuit of the heavenly self. Also, Caroline told us that it will awaken psychic abilities and help you recognize intuition and spiritual guidance."

Gideon slipped it onto her finger, but only as far as her knuckle. Onimia continued with the properties of the stone, an azurite, as he pushed it all the way to her hand.

"It calms you and will relieve mental stress. I'm not sure what dissolving any blocked energy means, but I figured you could use it with your sister coming to join us." She laughed when he did. "Native Americans valued the stone by using it to communicate with the spirit guides. The Mayans did too. We wanted you to have this, and the charm bracelet that goes with it, to help you with things that are going on in your life. We also want you to remember that no matter what, we're here for you."

They kissed her then, both of them taking her mouth, her throat, and her hands to their mouth and making love to it. She wasn't sure what made them stop, but when they both pulled back from her, she whimpered.

"Your sister is here." Gracie told Onimia to tell her to go away. "As much as I'd like to do that for you, we have to finish this with her. Then we'll finish what we started here as soon as she's gone. If you've a mind to."

"She's going to be a bitch. As usual." Gideon nodded. "And she's going to go right for the jugular too. There's no holding back with Cora. If she finds an opening, like this sham of a marriage, she'll throw it back at us."

Onimia kissed her on the nose as he stood up. "She won't find any sham should she look for it. The paperwork has been filed that says we married three days ago. Asher was there, as well as the rest of the brothers. The sisters-in-law were all witnesses, and my parents made us a dinner. If she asks, there are pictures that we can show her. It's very helpful having a witch in the family. There really aren't any pictures, but we have some that will tell her exactly what we want her to know. They're pictures of us at Christmas a few years ago, but Cora won't see that...she'll see a happily married couple having dinner with the family." With a quick kiss on the nose from them both, she watched them walk away.

They left her sitting there. She might have stayed there for the entire visit but for the children that came running into the house. And then the shrill voice of Cora. The children had more fun with her in one afternoon than they did the entire time that Cora had been their mom. And Gracie was going to make sure that they had a blast today too.

"What a place you have here, Mrs. Benson. My goodness, this must have set you back a great deal. Did you do this to impress me?" Sally turned and looked at her, shock all over her face. "It was unnecessary if you did. I'm only here to convince my mother and sister that the foolishness that they've been up to has gone on long enough."

"I don't impress anyone, child. And if I were you, I'd keep a civil tongue in my mouth or shut up. This is my home, and you are welcome here for now." Sally turned to the children and smiled at them. "Boys, there are some games and such in the play room. Asher put them in just today for me. I've been playing them for hours and having so much fun."

Sally took the boys to wherever the room was. Gracie knew for a fact that there wasn't such a room yesterday, and as far as she knew, Sally didn't give into games like most people did. She kept herself busy in other ways. Like canning and making jams and jellies.

"Well, Gracie, what do you have to say for yourself? Making me come all this way to get you back on track. I'm telling you right now, I don't have time for this. Nor do I care for the way that you and Mother have been treating me." Gracie said nothing; not that she didn't have plenty to say, but interrupting her sister when she was on a roll was useless. "These nice people have put up with you long enough. And now you've dragged Mother here. I demand that you come back home and we'll pretend that none of this happened. Hopefully none of my friends have gotten wind of this. It's embarrassing enough having the two of you around, much less flittering about like a bug to a light."

"You won't pretend to forget this for anything, Cora. For years from now, you'll bring up how you had to save the day by bringing Mom and me to heel." Cora started to say something and Gracie cut her off. "Shut up. I have the floor now. I'm not going back with you. I've put my house on the market and I'm selling it. I have a nice husband now, a good family that I actually enjoy being around, and I'm living my life the way that I want to."

Cora didn't like to be cut off nor told to shut up. She didn't actually like much of anything, but right now, Gracie didn't care. As she watched the anger roll over her sister's face, she knew just when she found a bit of flesh exposed and went for it.

"Do they know about how you're damaged?" Cora rubbed her hand over her belly and smiled. "Children are the only thing in the world that I love more than my husband. And they bring a certain kind of love to a marriage. Do they know that you won't be able to give them that?"

"Yes, we do. And you're not a nice person for bringing it up either." Cora turned to Gideon, no doubt to blast him, but took a step back when he towered over her. "Why don't we go into the living room, have a nice quiet conversation about your trip, and try to get along?"

Cora huffed at them, but pinched her lips closed. Mom took that moment to come into the room and hug her. Gracie wanted to slap Cora when she took a step back from Mom and did the same to her.

"My goodness, Mother, what have you been rolling in? You positively stink." Sally inhaled sharply and Gracie saw Jacob, a very nice man, doubling up his fist as if he wanted to hit Cora. But her mom, just as pretty as you please, hugged Cora anyway.

"I've been rolling in the shit out in the barn. You should do it sometime. But then.... Well, I guess you do that a great deal, don't you, Cora Jane? Hello, everyone, did I miss anything?" Onimia laughed first, then the rest of them did. It wasn't so much as an ice breaker as it was putting things right out there. Gracie moved into the living room, holding onto Gideon's arm, and the rest of them followed. It was going to be a long evening, if this was how it was to begin. Sitting on the sofa, the rest of the family, all of them, gathered around as well. Yes, she thought, this is going to be a long night.

She was surprised that William sat across the room from Cora. When she asked after her children, Mom told her they were fine. And of course, Cora had to go on about how she would be the judge about when her children were fine or not. When Jacob stood up, so did his sons, all twelve of them. It was going to be a showdown, she thought, and stood as well. Gideon stretched his neck until it popped twice before his dad spoke.

"This is my home. And being that, you will keep your tongue behind your teeth before I toss you out on your bottom. We invited you here to get to know you. Well, I have to tell you, you sure aren't making a good first impression. Now, as much as it pains me to say this, you are not a nice person." Cora stood up and Jacob told her to sit. She did so immediately. "Now. As I was saying, this is my house. You will, and I mean this, you will behave and stop picking at everyone, including my wife and children. Do you understand me?"

"I'm not doing anything wrong." Jacob nodded. "You must see what my mother and sister did to me."

"No, I don't see a durn thing. Now, why don't you wait, for just a moment or two, before you go jumping to conclusions? There ain't no reason for you to be making this sort of show when we ain't done nothing wrong but invite you here." Cora asked him why he was on Gracie's side. "She's married to my son. And even if she weren't, I think I'm a bit more inclined to like her kind of talking than yours. As it's been pointed out to you a bunch of times now, you're not a nice person."

Chapter 5

Onimia wasn't one to lose his temper much. Rarely did he let his head lead him into places that he didn't want to go. But right now, he wanted to take Cora Daniels outside and burn her to a crisp. Just like that, ridding the world of her sour disposition.

You okay? Gracie took his hand under the table as she spoke to him through their link. *Don't hurt her. Not that I don't want you to, but it wouldn't settle well with you should you eat her. Or whatever it was you were thinking of doing to her. She's bitter to the core, I think.*

You do know that she has everyone on edge, don't you? I mean, right now I think any one of my family would gladly murder her for you. Gracie smiled at him as she let go of his hand to pass the potatoes. *How on earth did you ever be in the same room with her when you were growing up?*

Believe it or not, she wasn't always like this. When we were kids she was sweet and we played all the time. Then she went on a vacation with one of her school friends when she was about ten or eleven. All the way to Paris and around the countryside for over a month. As soon as she returned, things became so different that Mom had her examined for some sort of infection. I think she got a taste for money and it went to her head. Onimia shook his head in disbelief. *I think she only married William because his family had money. Not a great deal, mind you, but enough for her to have a big house and nice cars. My mom and I, we didn't have because we saw no reason to spend on things we didn't need. Money in the bank was more important, to us anyway.*

He didn't want to say anything, but he knew for a fact that the child that Cora was using against her sister didn't exist. And the boys weren't her husband's. It was doubtful that even Cora knew who the father of them was. Onimia had touched the children several times to be sure of it. He also knew that they were unhappy, not just the boys but the husband as well, and that the fighting between their parents was making the older one ill, and the youngest was having nightmares. Partly due to their mother...the rest was how depressed William was all the time.

What is it you know? He glanced at Gideon when he spoke to him. *You know something. I can tell. And just to let you know, I'm going to murder this woman before the day is done.*

He laughed, then covered it with a cough when Cora glared at him. Onimia wasn't afraid of her...quite the opposite, as a matter of fact. But he didn't like her. She was vicious, and she had a mean streak in her that would get her into trouble soon enough.

I was just thinking about the boys. They're not William's. Gideon said that he knew that. *Do you think that Gracie does? I think Jules is aware of it. Now there is a wonderful woman. I'm glad that she's nothing like Cora.*

Me too. I thought for sure that Dad was going to hurt Cora. Onimia told him what Gracie had just told him. *Well, we'll keep an eye on her. I think she's holding her own very well.*

Yes, me too. Onimia tuned in to the conversation around him, just in time to hear Jules telling the table about her trip. *We should see if she'd like to stay here. She's aware of what we are now and that we're both her mates. It might be good for them both to be around positive people for a change.*

Good idea.

Onimia decided to talk to Asher about a house in town. That way they'd have their privacy and so would Jules. Even if she didn't want to hang around here, she could have a home that she could land in when she wanted to visit.

"When are you coming back home? Either of you?" Cora didn't look at anyone when she asked, but he knew it was aimed at her mom. "I can't tell you how much trouble you've caused me by just taking off like you did, Mother. I won't stand for that. You became a grandmother when I had my children, and I would like for you to start taking that job seriously. Like being home when I want you there."

"Well then, I guess it sucks to be you. Because like Gracie, I've put my house on the market." Jules smiled at Cora when she sat there staring at her. "Do close your mouth, dear, you're showing off all your caps."

Her mouth closed with an auditable snap. Onimia laughed, this time not caring to cover it up with a cough. He was making an enemy and he didn't care. So long as Gracie was all right, then he was as well.

"What do you mean, you're selling your house? Have the two of you gone off your rockers? You can't do that. I want you at home so that you can watch my sons." Jules said nothing but passed the platter of chicken to Cora. "I don't eat that sort of food and you know it. And if you plan on being around for a while, I would suggest that you stop eating fatty foods too. Do you want to continue to be overweight your whole life? Answer my question, Mother. I won't have you doing things like selling your only home. And if you think you're going to come running to me when you need a place to stay, then you can forget that as well."

"My goodness, Cora, you act like Mom and I can't make a move without your say-so. I don't know if you realize this or not, but we're both grown women, and don't need nor even want your approval. I, for one, am excited about this next phase of my life." Cora asked her what that was going to be. "Being married again. Having a good home, a place to rest my head. And if Mom wants to live around here, I'd gladly pay for her a home."

"I won't help." Gracie said it wasn't necessary. "You don't have that sort of money. Cain was a loser. You only have a home because he did the one smart thing in his life before dying, and that was putting money down for that shack. And it was a shack too, and you know it."

"I know nothing of the sort. And you didn't like him, did you? Is it because he wouldn't sleep with you? He told me all about you coming on to him. In fact, we had a good laugh about it." Gracie smiled, but it was cold and hard. "You should be ashamed of yourself for making a move on my husband. How many others have there been?"

"What the fuck are you talking about?" Cora looked like she'd been caught with her hand not only in the cookie jar, but also with her other hand in the bank. "I've never.... If he told you that, then he was lying. He came on to me. I told him you were my sister."

"We had cameras in our house." It lay there, that statement. So much so that Cora was able to stand and sit three times before Gracie continued. "I also am aware that there is no child in your belly. And that neither of the two boys you carried are his children. And William knows now too, don't you?"

William didn't move. Onimia just noticed that there wasn't any food on his plate, nor had he taken a drink of the tea that was in his glass. It was as if he were frozen in place… that some news had been put to him prior to dinner, and he was too full digesting it rather than the food on the table.

"William? You aren't listening to this sort of shit, are you? I mean, you know that Gracie has always been a liar and that—"

"We're broke." No one said a word, and Onimia noticed that Asher's fork was still between his mouth and the plate in front of him. "The credit cards are maxed out. The boys' private school is demanding their payments, along with the cars and the credit cards. I was a fool to let you take care of the money. A fool."

"This is nothing to talk about now, William. We're talking about my mother and sister and their lack of helping us." Cora looked around the table, her face pale and her voice a little higher than it had been. "He's not right on that. We have all the money in the world. The payments he's talking about, I've already taken care of them."

"The boys aren't mine, just as your sister said. I didn't know for sure, but when Mike was sick a few months ago, they did a blood test on him to see if he had meningitis. He didn't, but then they did a test on my blood too, to see if I had whatever he had. We'd been ill for several days, the two of us. They discovered that our blood didn't match. A few days later, I took Connor in and had him tested too. Four days later, I went in and was cut so that there would be no more pretend children from me. Then you told me that there was

71

going to be another child, one that isn't any more real than the money you've been taking from me." William looked at her. "You've been sleeping around since we've been married. And so you know, I knew about Cain too. He came to me and told me that day you'd done it."

"He came on to me. I can't believe this. You have to believe me, William. I would never do that to you. As for the children not being yours, that just insane. Of course they're yours. You need to stop that line of thinking—"

"Even if there was a child, I don't know how it could be mine. After you told me that you were pregnant, I went to the doctor and made sure that I couldn't father any children. And he told me that it was impossible, that he'd taken care of it. And before you deny that too, I saw two more doctors and they told me the same. That child you told me you carry, it's not mine." William looked at Gracie, his eyes full of tears, his face pale. "You are going to be very happy, Gracie. You're a very nice person that deserves the very best."

"Thank you, William." He stood up then and looked around the room. "Please don't leave. We'll have a nice dinner, then you can stay here should you want to. Cora will be taken back to the hotel."

"No I will not. I'm staying with my husband. What are you doing, Gracie? Trying to steal my husband from me because you think that you can? Well, I have news for you. He's mine until I say differently." Cora stood up too, her body hard with anger. "I will see you dead before I let you come between us. Unlike Cain, my husband provides for us. He gives me what I want, when I want it, and he doesn't try and make a living out of taking pictures that no one cares about. Christ, he was better off dying like he did. At least I can assume now that he left you with a little cash."

"Forty million." Cora sat down then. "Forty million in insurance. Then when we sued the hospital and doctors, I came out with just under sixty million more. That wasn't the end of the money I got from all this. There was the car seat manufacturers for Beth's seat. That netted me just under one hundred million. You would have thought that it would have been less, what with me not being able to love her as much as you did your sons, as you told me that day you came to visit me in the hospital. I think you said that since she'd only been a girl and only a baby, my love for her hadn't blossomed like yours had. You have no idea how much you hurt me then. And now you've managed to surpass that hurt into something I don't think I'll ever be able to forgive you for."

"You have that much money? Why didn't you say so? Damn it, Gracie, I could have helped you with that." Gracie laughed. "What is so funny about that? Christ, you're a horrible person. I don't—"

"Enough." Asher stood up and looked at them. "Take Gracie to the kitchen, please. William too. We're going to have a conversation with Cora here."

"No." Onimia stood up and looked at Asher. "She's leaving, right now. Either on her own or I take her. Either way, she's done here."

"I will not leave here until my mother tells me when she's coming home." Onimia looked at Jules when everyone else did. "Mother. I think you've stayed here long enough. It's time for you to return home. This is just stupid. If you're trying to upset me, then you've done it. But enough is enough. You're to come home right now and stay there. If I have to, I'll take your car from you so that you can't just take off on a whim again. You've made my life very difficult, and I've had about enough."

73

"As far as I'm concerned, Cora, I am home. And as far as making your life difficult, that is all on you. I'm happy, which for some reason I thought you'd be happy for me to find that out. But it's all about you and has been for too many years for me to care anymore." She looked over at Sally. "You have to give me the recipe for these green beans. I'm thinking that it's because they're fresh, but they are the best I've ever eaten."

Onimia didn't wait for an answer. He moved toward Cora and was surprised to see William helping him move her toward the door. She was screaming the entire time about how she wasn't going to be treated this way as she was stuffed into the limo, and the driver told to take her to the hotel to pack. When she was gone, Onimia looked at the other man.

"I don't have a pot to piss in. I've found out some things recently that I had no idea that Cora was doing. I've lost my job, my home, as well as my reputation. Not that it was all that wonderful anyway, but no one will hire me now." Onimia said he'd help. "I don't want to impose, I really don't, but I don't think the boys will want anything to do with her. I've been talking to them, you see. And if you could see your way into helping me, you have no idea how grateful I'd be to you. Thank you."

"We'll help. And there's a job too. I can tell that you've been hurt by this. I don't know everything you do, but there is a great deal that she's been doing behind your back." Onimia would help, even if William didn't have the boys. "You come on into my parents' house and we'll figure this out."

"Thank you. I don't know what I'd do.... She's been getting worse and worse all the time. Then this with the kids.... My oldest, he's afraid of her." That wasn't good, he thought. "I don't want anything to do with her. They might not be my sons, but I've checked...I can still keep them as my own."

Onimia went back into the house with the other man. His family had been busy, it seemed. Not only was Cora's place setting missing, but the boys had joined them, and now there was laughter around the table too. He loved his family, more than he could ever say.

~~~

Cora got out of the limo even as he slid to a stop. She was pissed, and she was sure that her rantings were going to be reported back to the Bensons. As she entered the establishment, she was stopped at the front desk and asked to come to an office. She told the person that she didn't have time right this moment.

"I'm afraid that I'm going to have to insist that you come with me, Mrs. Daniels. There is a matter of your room." She asked what was wrong with her room. "It's no longer available for you."

"Excuse me? I am here until Friday. And since this is only Monday, I have a few more days. Not as if I had any other choice where I stay, but that's what was set up for myself and my family." The woman told her that there had been a change of plans. "What sort of change? I made no such changes. You know what, I don't care. Take it up with the people who set this up, but I'm not leaving."

"The Bensons called and they're not happy with you, apparently." She stood there, wondering what was going on when the woman spoke again. "The Bensons said that they were no longer paying for the room for you after tonight. That after that, you'll have to either leave or pay yourself. I'm sorry to have to tell you out here in the public, but I did try and take—"

"What do you mean, they've decided not to pay for my room any longer? They said I'd be here until Friday. They

75

cannot renege on that deal. I want to speak to the owner of this place. I have a few more things to tell them about how this hotel is below standards." The woman said that the Bensons owned the hotel. "Are you fucking kidding me? They own the place, and that gives them the right to throw me out?"

"Ma'am, I'm going to have to ask you to keep your voice down and watch your language." Cora told her to fuck off. "One more outburst like that, and I will call the police."

Cora wasn't in the mood to stand there and take this shit. Slapping the woman, she told her to get out of her face and turned to leave. She was going to figure out a way to rate this place so that no one, not one of her friends, would come here. Not that they'd be stuck in a place like this, but she was going to make sure that no one did. As she made her way to the elevators, two security guards came to stand with her.

"What the fuck do you want?" They told her they were there to help her pack. "I'm not leaving, so you can go about your business, buddy, and leave me alone. I have the room all to myself now, and I'm going to party it up."

"I'm sorry, ma'am, but we're not going to allow you to do that. The police are on their way as well." She asked him for what. "Assaulting another person, not leaving when you were asked. There are lots of reasons that they've been called in."

"I'll pay for the room then." She wasn't sure how she was going to manage that. She knew that the money for the cards had gone to shopping sprees and luncheons with friends. "Tell me how much it's going to be."

"That's no longer an option." She wasn't going to allow anyone to dictate to her what she was going to do and when. It was bad enough that her husband had been going behind her back about crap. These people were going to pay. "Mrs.

Daniels, you'll have to leave now."

"No, I'm not. I'm going to leave when I'm damned good and ready. You'll just have to explain to the Bensons, who are not very nice people that would throw a pregnant woman out on her ass, that I'm not leaving." The man just rolled on his feet. "Are you stupid? I said that I'm not leaving. You go on about whatever it is you're supposed to be doing and leave me alone."

"You're going out the easy way or the hard, miss. I don't really care which. As for the Bensons, they're the nicest, most generous people you'll ever meet. And if they want you out, then I'm thinking that you did something powerfully wrong for them to tell me that. So either way, you're leaving here, simply because they said so."

She looked over his shoulder and saw the police. Finally, someone with half a brain to help her.

"This man is detaining me for no reason." She looked at the guard. "That means, in case you didn't know, that you were stopping me without any reason to do so. And they're going to throw me out of this place simply on the say-so of the all mighty Bensons. I want you to arrest them all."

"I know what it means. Believe it or not, I have a college education. And I'm not going to take you in on the say-so of the Bensons. You assaulted someone." She doubted that he'd even finished high school and told him so. "Whatever you want to believe, you go right on ahead."

The elevator opened its doors and she slipped inside. She was hoping to get into her room and lock the door before they realized she was gone. But before she could even press the button on the dumb thing, not only the guards but the police joined her. They talked around her, acting as if she wasn't even in the cubical with them.

"Did you see that game last night? Man, that was a close one. It was nice of the Bensons to allow us to come on up to the big house to watch it with them. And the food." She got it now, they were on the take and the Bensons were paying them. "My wife and I had a wonderful time. And the mayor said that he'd not had better company in a long while."

"Is this entire town on the take? Good Christ, the Bensons must be made of fucking money." The cop who had been talking laughed. "Oh please, let me in on the joke. I could use a good laugh before I call in the Feds and have them come here for corruption and such."

"The Bensons are the richest people in the world, I think. And they would never stoop to paying off anyone. They're good people with good hearts. Unlike some that we know." All of them nodded. She asked him if he meant her. "If the shoe fits, I guess."

She was furious, but venting to these people would do her no good. Sitting on the bed when she entered her room, she realized that it had not only been cleaned, but it looked as if someone had come in and taken away her husband's and children's things. Which reminded her, she didn't have her sons.

"Where are my children?" No one looked at her as they picked up her packed bags. "You put that right down. I've told you that I'm not leaving. What is wrong with you people? Are you all sharing the same brain or something? I am not leaving here until I say so."

"You're leaving, and so you know, you're under arrest as well." She asked him on what charges. "Assault, as I have told you twice now. I'm sure that somewhere between here and the jail you'll be able to drum up some more. Now, if you'd come along quietly, Mrs. Daniels, we can get this—"

"I swear to Christ, if any of you touch me, I'm going to make some phone calls." They didn't ask her about what, so she decided to enlighten them. "I'm going to tell everyone that I know that you hurt me. That you treated me badly, and with me being pregnant."

"We're all wearing body cameras with sound. Even Carl here, he's wearing one too." She looked at the security guard who had approached her first. He pointed to his camera. The cop continued. "So that's not going to work. And there are cameras in the hall and elevator that were on when we got in. So again, that won't work. You've been told, numerous times, that you're to be put out. No one has touched nor hurt you in any way whatsoever. Now, you come along and we won't have to get you on resisting arrest too."

She went with them. Really, she had no choice in the matter. They had her things, including her purse. There was no one for her to call either. William was being childish, and her sister wasn't very nice either. Then there was her mother. Cora doubted that she'd come to help her even if she was on fire. There was bad blood there too.

Cora hated her family. Not hated, that word had no real meaning to her. She disliked them. They didn't do what she wanted them to and they embarrassed her. All the time. She dared not invite them to have lunch with her at the club, like other women did. Cora knew that they'd say the wrong thing, or heaven forbid, wear something that wasn't up to her standards, and that would make her the butt of many jokes and jabs for years to come. No, there was no hating her mother and sister, but she certainly didn't care for them.

When Cora was in the jail cell, after being searched by the female police officer, she sat on the bed and tried to think where things had gone wrong. Yes, she had spent the money unwisely, but that didn't make her a bad person. Besides, William would recoup it for her. He was a good man. If he was mad about the boys not being his, she'd take care of that as well. She'd give him permission to have a few himself, and that should satisfy him. Having affairs was a way of life for the rich. No one slept with the same person night after night like they used to. And as for the kids not being her husband's? That shouldn't have mattered to him either, not when she'd carried them to term and had put his name on the certificate for him. People were getting funny ideas in their heads, and she wasn't going to stand for it.

Cora asked to use the phone when she realized that she needed to put her foot down starting now. She'd tell William to come here, and she'd tell him what was going on. Without all those other people around, she'd be able to convince him of anything she needed. Especially about the job and the boys. There was no telling what sort of things they were putting in his head. Her mother and sister would be all over this, making her the bad guy again and again.

"You can as soon as we get you booked." She sat down again and wondered what difference it was going to make. She wasn't going to be here long anyway. "Also, Mrs. Daniels, I'm to tell you that you'll have to make your own transportation home now. The Bensons aren't going to do that for you. Not after the way you treated their sister-in-law."

"She's my sister. Dumb as they come too. And I can treat her any way I see fit, they'll have to learn that. Have you met her? She's stupid if she thinks I'm going to believe that her first husband left her that well off." She tried to get the pounding in her head to stop. "Look, tell them as soon as William comes here to get me, we'll leave. And on their plane. They brought us all here, and now they'll take care that we get home. Of all the thoughtless.... Tell Gracie I want to see her and Mother too. I don't have time for this shit, and they'll straighten things out for us. This is all a big misunderstanding on their part."

He simply walked away. Cora was going to have to put down some rules that she would expect them to follow. If her family was going to continue on this line of thinking, she was going to have to go to the extreme. She'd been nice until now, but they were getting out of control. There was no way she'd done a damned thing wrong that would warrant this sort of treatment. She'd show them, damn it.

Chapter 6

Anthony held his love's hand. They were both so nervous that he could actually feel it from Eve. When she touched her fingers to his cheek, he felt her warmth rather than the touch and that was enough for him. Especially after being away from her for so long.

"Do you suppose they'll like us?" He laughed, Anthony just couldn't help himself. "I know that you think because we're their parents that they have to, but we did leave them with strangers."

"Very kind and loving strangers. Besides, they weren't strangers to them after they were born, love, and I think that they only survived because of Jacob and Sally." Eve nodded. "I'm excited to see them all. Not being able to touch them is difficult, but seeing them is so special."

They were meeting them at midnight in front of the castle. It had been centuries since either of them had been there, and now that they were, they could only marvel at how much had been done to the falling stone. Anthony had wanted to walk the halls, but the building was still under repair, mostly to the inner walls, and he was afraid of getting trapped there again. It had been his death, to be inside when the walls had come down upon him.

He knew too that the magic was slowing now that the walls were up. The earth had given all that she could to get them up, and moving them around was draining not just on her but every living creature around. She would work only in bits so that nothing would be harmed by it. Anthony touched the walls, giving a little of what he had left, and the earth thanked him. It was a good feeling, having magic still after he'd been murdered.

"There they come." He looked in the direction that Eve was pointing and saw only their sons. The six hatchlings of them were bigger men than Anthony had ever dreamed they'd be. "Where are the others? I thought we'd get to see them all."

When he'd spoken to Onimia and Gideon the other day, they'd told him about how they were getting things finished at the castle. How excited they were to have moved his body to be with his mom. It was what brought them to this point. Their love for each other had awakened them in a way that neither of them had seen in their dreams of the future. One heart beating in a great dragon.

"I don't think they're coming." Eve sounded so disappointed that he wanted to hold her. He could touch her, even kiss her, but it was strange, this affair they were having. "Oh Anthony, I so wanted to see them all. And where are Jacob and Sally?"

"There. There they come now." The others were behind their sons. Holding back, he could see. Then it occurred to him what they were doing. "I think they're waiting for us to speak to our sons in private, love. Give us a few moments

84

with them alone."

"No. I want them all here now." She waved them over, and when they didn't heed her needs, he realized they might not be able to see them as yet. He looked at his son Onimia and smiled.

"They cannot see you. None of the others can either." He had feared that. Anthony was as disappointed as he could be. "Would it be all right if I bring our mate to us? She might be the one that makes it happen so that they can see you."

It took several minutes for Gracie to come to them. She was nervous, he could almost taste it on her. But when she came forward with the rest of the family, Anthony got his first look at his granddaughters too.

"Oh my, Eve, she looks of you." He looked at Asher when he drew in a sharp breath. It was then that he knew they could all see him. "My goodness, Asher, you look of your father. Stronger, I think, bigger for sure. You're a good king, then?"

"I'm trying to be. I don't have a clue what I'm about. But...it's so good to meet you, sir. You've no idea how much we wanted this." Anthony nodded and asked to see the girls better, his granddaughters. "They're named for the two of you. This is Sally Ann, mine and Kiaran's daughter. And this is Eve Marie, daughter to Jed and Zak. I know that Ann isn't your name, but it was as close as we could get without calling her Anthony."

"'Tis a fine name. One to be proud of. They're lovely, aren't they? My goodness, we're grandparents, Eve. Just look at them." He wanted to touch them. Hold one of them, both of them to his heart and feel their warmth. "We have magic for them, to help them in the coming years. All the children of our sons will have it, and their children as well."

"If you'd not mind, sir, I'd like to try something." He

looked at Gracie, such a wonderfully lovely woman, and nodded. "I think I can make it so you can hold her. I'm not sure it'll work, but I saw it on a movie once. And, well, I can't think it'll hurt to try, right?"

"Whatever you wish, we'd very much like to try." She nodded at him and asked who would like to be first. "Eve, my lady wife. That way if it works for only a little while, she'll be able to tell me what it felt like."

When Gracie stepped behind Eve, he wanted to tell her to be careful, but she was as sure of herself as he was with his own powers. Gracie might be new to the magic that came to her, but she was doing well with it. While she tried her hand at her idea, he looked at the young man that had joined their family. Young Mark.

"You have a brownie, I see. He is good to you?" Mark nodded and smiled. It was like seeing the sun again. "He is a good man, Peck. I remember him from long ago. There is something in the castle keep for you. I'll let Peck know where it is so that he might retrieve it for you. It's a sword that was —"

"Anthony?" He looked at Eve and saw that Gracie's plan had worked. His lady love was holding the child in her arms, and she was sobbing. "She's so tiny. I've...I've never held one of my own children, but I think this is so much better. Look at her stare at me."

Gracie had entered her body. Anthony knew not how that had come about, but he was overwhelmed with emotion just seeing Eve cuddle the child over her heart. As they stood there, the two of them, he felt something touch him and cried out when someone entered his body as well. It was his son. He could feel his dragon at his back.

Touch her, Father. Hold your other granddaughter, Eve. He

reached for the babe when she was put out for him and cried out again, this time in pure pleasure and love. Kiaran didn't speak again, but helped him become whole. As he held his granddaughter, he gave her some of the magic that he still had when he'd been killed. But this, this right now, was perhaps the greatest joy he'd ever had. To hold one of his children's children made him think he could leave this earth a very happy man.

They passed the girls and even Mark back and forth. Touching their sons, even those of Sally and Jacob as much as they could. He knew that his host was weakening, but Kiaran said that he'd take a nap, this was so worth the exhaustion. Anthony didn't know if this would ever work again so he held him, just for now.

As the sun started to rise, they knew that the magic that held them there would weaken. The witching hour, midnight, had given them more than they ever dreamed possible. Anthony spoke to Peck, told him what he wanted from him, then as the boys moved away, taking the children with them, he looked at Jacob and Sally.

"You have done better than we could have ever hoped for in this." Jacob bowed and Sally nodded. "We have more for you. Magic as well. There are books I should like for you to gather. They are in the castle, but hidden deep within the stone."

"We can get them for you. Gracie has been gathering the witches' books, ones that were murdered long ago. They come to her almost daily and tell her where to find theirs." Anthony was surprised by that, but said nothing. It was a good thing, not to worry about a book falling into the wrong hands. "We've missed you, my lord. I hope that this isn't a one-time thing. You must see the children grow."

"We will, but not always where you can see us. It's hard to stay here, on this side, so that you can view us." Jacob said he could understand that. "You've never asked me what this would do for you. Not once, in all the time you've been coming to this castle, did you wonder what you were to get from my asking you two to do this."

Sally looked at Jacob before speaking. "You've paid us well and beyond what we could have ever hoped for, my lord. We have twelve boys to keep us company. Grandchildren coming now as well. A roof over our heads, and now we have more than enough food for our bellies." She looked around and so did he. "There is no need for payment, nor will there ever be. We have more, much more than that in the way of love and happiness. We've no need for anything else, save that."

Faeries and other forest creatures were surrounding them now. All of them standing there, watching the couple that had been here longer than he had ever hoped. Anthony saw his brother-in-law, Daniel, was there, his armor bright in the morning sunlight. Stepping toward them, all of them came to him. It was wonderful, seeing so many people that he never thought to speak to again.

He and Eve spoke to the others that had come. His mind, however, was still on a payment that he could bestow upon the people who had made this all possible. If Jacob and Sally hadn't agreed, all the other work, the foundation that they had laid for their sons to be safe, would have been for nothing. As they were making their way back to their cave, he spoke to Eve about his wants and needs.

"I'm sure that you shall think of something grand for them, but I think that they'd be upset that you don't think that living forever and having such wonderful children was enough." He nodded, his mind not letting go now that he had it in this head. "You could always give them tails and let them be fish in the great river behind the castle."

"Nay, that will not work. Jacob is afeared of water, and Sally, now that she's back, has no desire to be.... You have teased me." She laughed, a sound that he had missed more than he could have said. "I love you, lady wife. More than anything in this world we travel in."

"And I you, the blood of my heart. You are the only reason that I would take the chance to walk among the living. We shall think of something, but you should really ask them, my love. They will be happy with just having such a good life."

By the time they were at their bodies again, they were both exhausted. To have been so real for this long was something that they'd not prepared for, but seeing their family, all of them, it was beyond what he'd ever hoped or even wished for. As he closed his eyes, he reached for Eve's hand and felt it curl in his. Love. It was what made death so much easier to stand.

~~~

Gideon wasn't sure how to begin. Gracie had gone to take a bath, to soak away her sister's meanness, and they were in their bedroom waiting for her to return. He was sure that as soon as either one of them touched her, she'd be upset with them. Taking it slow was what was needed here, but all he wanted to do was strip her down and take her hard against the wall. He looked over at Onimia when he sighed heavily.

"We should do something." Gideon asked him what. "I don't know, but I feel like a vulture waiting for a piece of meat to be dropped in front of me."

"That's about right." He grinned when Onimia did. "Should we just join her? Be naked in the bed when she comes out? I haven't any idea how to start this with her."

"You've had sex before, haven't you?" Gideon said that he had, but this wasn't the same. "Why not? I mean, is it because of me?"

"No. Not because of you. What a thing to say. No, it's because she's our mate and she's been alone for so long." He didn't think that was right either and tried again. "We'll have to go slowly, right? Make her know that we love her more than anything. And that we're not in this only for the sex."

"Yes, that's a good point." When someone cleared their throat, they both looked up at Gracie, who was standing there wearing a towel, her hair dripping wet. "We were talking about you."

"So I heard. And have you come to any conclusions as yet? Just to give you a heads up, I've never had sex with two men before. Do you have it with each other too?" Gideon said that he wasn't sure, but he had no desire to make love to Onimia. "Okay. Then why are you sitting out here and not in the bathtub with me?"

Onimia stood up first, then Gideon did. Where to start seemed to be taken out of their hands. But still, this would be their first time and he wanted it to be special. Something that she'd enjoy from them both. So, instead of following her into the bathroom, for now anyway, he pulled her into his arms and kissed her.

He had kissed her before. She tasted of flowers and honey. Gideon thought her skin was the thing that all bees were attracted to. But this time, with her mouth under his, she tasted different. Her breath was tastier. Her tongue danced along his as he touched her. When he felt her breast in his hand, filling it fully, he looked at Onimia who was just behind her, tasting her neck and shoulder.

The towel was in a heap at her feet. Gideon stripped his clothing off, making sure to not rush her as he was at it, but her hand wrapped around his cock, and it was all he could do not to come all over her. When she bent in front of him, taking him into her mouth, he watched as Onimia ran his hands up and down her spine as he held his own cock.

"Take me, Onimia. I want to feel your cock inside of me while I taste Gideon." He moved then, his cock poised at her entrance, and when she pushed back at him, he knew that the moment Onimia filled her, the instant he took their mate, and Gideon knew he was going to come and come hard.

His cock was painfully full. Gideon wanted it to last, to make her come before them, but watching her being fucked by his other half, the way his hands molded and moved over her skin, made it harder and harder for Gideon to think beyond coming right now. And when she cupped his balls, giving them a slight twist, he cried out his release at the same time that Onimia did when he came too.

They made their way to the bed. Her body was dewy, whether from the bath or them he wasn't sure, but she was touching them as much as they were her. And when she told them she was close, all he could think about was seeing her face when she released.

The bed was large enough. When Asher had helped them with the house, using his magic to make it be perfect for them, he enlarged not only the room but the pieces of furniture in it as well. The bed was square, and they could stretch out on it in any direction. Right now, with her in the middle of the bed, he and Onimia lay at her sides.

"Please. I need some relief." Onimia moved down her body, kissing and nipping at her flesh as he went. Gideon suckled at her breasts, her navel, and any other place that he could touch her. When she cried out, he looked down her beautiful body and saw Onimia between her legs, her thighs up around his ears as he devoured her. As her body tensed, her breast became hard and she cried out, screaming both their names as she came. Gideon thought for so long as he lived, he'd never forget the look on her face when she did.

Onimia feasted on her for several minutes. She came so many times, every time lovelier than the last while he tasted her. Kissing her lips, her nipples and her ears, he told her of his love for her, the way she made him feel like a man of worth. And when Onimia said it was Gideon's turn, he kissed her again, tasting her sweetness once more before he tasted her wetness.

Gracie tasted of Onimia, magic, and even him. Fucking her with his tongue, he marveled that she was theirs, and that she would be with them for the rest of their long lives. Needing to feel her wrapped around him, he moved up her body and between her legs. Gideon knew that he'd not last long. She was hot, her body ripe for him. Looking into her eyes, he filled her slowly, stretching her for his cock as she begged him for more.

Onimia was on her chest while her fingers dug deeply into his ass. While he couldn't see what they were doing, he could hear enough to know that they were both enjoying themselves. When Onimia moved, his body sliding off of Gracie, Gideon leaned over her and fucked her as hard as he could, moving her up the bed as he did so.

"Come inside of me, Gideon, please. Complete me as Onimia has." His cock seemed to fill tighter and his body tenser. As he pounded her, giving her all he had, he leaned to her breast and bit down. As soon as her blood filled his mouth, he came so hard that he saw dragons. Small dragons that swam around his head.

When he moved—when he could—Onimia took her. Gideon thought himself spent, his body unable to give even a little more. But watching the two of them, being together as they should, his heart filled and his body hardened again. These two, they were his life.

Onimia cried out twice, his body bowed back as he came. Gideon thought it was the most beautiful thing that he'd ever seen in all his life. And as his other half dropped on her, rolling to his side at the last minute, Gideon curled around her back as Onimia did her front. Closing his eyes, he was asleep in seconds.

He saw the woman; she was far away but he knew who she was. Gideon wasn't sure how he knew, but her name, Delia, seemed to rush over him when she turned and looked at him. There was an aura about her, something that told him that she wasn't a nice person. Or, and for some reason this struck him as truer, she was going to be a great deal of trouble for not just him but his entire family. As soon as that thought entered his head, he knew it to be true.

"Hello." He nodded, not sure if this was his dream or hers, or why he was here. "I'm going to tell you something that you cannot tell anyone else. Not even your mate."

Again, he said nothing. He realized that she said mate, not mates, so he simply nodded again. Her smile didn't make him feel like he was getting something nice bestowed upon him. So when she put out her hand to touch him, he took a step back.

"So untrusting, aren't you? No matter. You'll see that I mean you no harm." Gideon looked around them, careful to keep an eye on Delia. "Do you not like this place? It was hard for me to figure out what you'd feel trusting about, so I made

93

this for you. So calming."

The walls, or whatever they were, were stark white. The floor, ceiling, and table and chairs were as well. As he looked behind the woman, he saw Lelani. And when she put her finger to her lips, he was suddenly very afraid.

Don't talk to me, but listen. This is Delia, black witch to the king Rupert. Helena was her pupil, but they never got along well. But right now that's not important. Just don't speak to her. Not even to agree or disagree with anything that she wants. He wasn't sure if he could speak to her through their link, so didn't. *Good boy, Gideon. And in the event you're wondering, your mates are here with you. However, they cannot be seen by her or you. To keep them safe.*

"You're not answering me, dragon. Why is that? Did you know of me?" He wasn't sure if he could shake his head so he took another step back from Delia. "You're very frustrating. I only came to help you, and the others like you. Come. You want to help your family, do you not? They're the best looking dragons I've ever seen."

"Delia." The witch turned when the man spoke. It was King Anthony and his queen. "This one is not for you. You are to leave him alone or I shall come after you again."

Delia looked at him, then back at the king and queen. He saw fear in her eyes...though it was quickly replaced with anger, but he knew that she was afraid of Anthony. Lelani stood to his right, and Gideon knew that his mates were on his left side. Comfort washed over him as the four of them stood there.

"You're dead. I know this. I saw it with my own eyes when you were felled." Anthony laughed, as did Eve. "This is not fair, Dragon King. You are dead. There is no other but the ones that this man holds."

94

"Are you so sure about that? You don't look it. In fact, I think you look as if you're not sure if you even have the right king." Delia looked back at Gideon, then at Anthony again. "Are you sure that I'm king of dragons? Are you even sure, with your own eyes, that I am dead?"

"You confuse me." He laughed again, but when she turned to Gideon, he felt Lelani stiffen. "Show me your true self, dragon. I wish to see you."

Do not move. He wasn't planning on it. *When I tell you to, I want you to raise your arms above your head and call on the white witch, Caroline. Say this, just like I tell you. 'Come to me, white witches of all time. Caroline and your coven, come to me.'*

Lifting his arms up, he said the quote to himself twice before he opened his mouth. Before he could say a word out loud, Delia started screaming and holding her ears. Gideon then woke in his own bed, his mates sitting next to him on the bed and Lelani standing at the foot.

Chapter 7

Cora paced the tiny cell and tried to think why she was even here. Yes, she had hit someone that she shouldn't have. But she had been angry, and everyone knew that pregnant women were hormonal. Other than that, there wasn't really any reason for her to be in jail. She went to the bars again and called out for some help.

The woman coming down the long hall had something in her hands, and Cora thought it was a cell phone. What she wouldn't give to have one of those right now. Not only would she be posting pictures of her ill treatment, but she'd be begging her friends not to forget her. Cora knew that she was well respected and loved, but since they didn't know where she was, they couldn't be here for her.

"Yes, I was wondering when someone was going to let me out of here. I'll apologize if I have to, but I want you to know that I only hit that person because I couldn't murder them. If you think about it, I should be applauded rather than put in jail." The woman in front of her just stared. "Did you hear me? I want you to answer my question."

97

"You didn't ask anything. You stated a whole bunch of things, but there wasn't a question. And in the event you do ask, again, you're not getting out of here until your court hearing. I guess you've been causing an uproar in two different states. And don't ask me again about a phone. You get one call, which you have used, and you don't get another one until after the hearing. We've gone over this time and time again." The woman handed her a sheet of paper. "I'm to find out what you want for breakfast. And all you're going to get, Mrs. Daniels, is the stuff that is listed. We're not running a restaurant here, and I'm not going to run out and get you something that's not on there. Pick one thing from each column."

Cora handed it back to her without looking at it. "I want orange juice, freshly squeezed, whole wheat toast with butter, not margarine, and a poached egg. One, and it must be runny or it's going to upset me." The woman, Cora couldn't be bothered to learn her name, told her that nothing she said was on the menu today. "I don't care. That's what I want. Now you scurry along and get it for me. Along with someone that can tell me when I'm being released."

Turning away, her choices made, she sat on the bed. Yesterday she'd wanted the same thing, and she was given half a bagel that had seeds on it, a glass of disgusting juice that she wasn't sure what it was, and a cold cup of coffee. She supposed that regular people, convicts, would enjoy such a treat, but not her. She wasn't used to such shabby meals.

Cora was sick of being treated like the bad guy. It wasn't as if she'd killed anyone. Just a small slap to someone wasn't worth getting their panties in a twist about. The woman had embarrassed her and pissed her off. As she sat there, waiting for her food to be delivered, she thought of her latest lover.

Dom.

He wasn't very smart, but then no man was really. It took a strong woman to make them into what they needed to be. And while her husband was a smart man in some areas, he was extremely naïve when it came to others. Like making love.

Dom had a big dick, and he knew how to use it. The problem was, while he could use it well, she had to tell him each move to make, when to touch her, and worse yet, how to make her come. She thought, at times, that having a vibrator would do her more good than a man. But now she was going to have his baby. Fucker had told her that he was fixed. She was going to have to insist on seeing medical records from now on.

William had gotten fixed. She hadn't known that. It sure did put a crimp in her plans to get him to go along with her ideas. Like having more children. Children, she knew, held a family together. And she was sure that from now on he'd not let her have his paycheck. Well, she was sure there were ways around that, but she was too angry to figure them out at the moment. Hearing the door open, she stood and started talking before she saw who was coming.

"I swear to you; you people certainly do take your time in getting something for someone to eat. What was the delay this time? The cook was ill? You had to go and pull the egg from the chicken?" She looked at the man in front of her and nearly missed that it was her husband. "William, thank goodness you've come to get me out of here. I need for you to take some names down of people. They need to be reprimanded. What did you do to yourself? You look like you've only just rolled out of bed and pulled on the first thing you touched. Regardless of who it belonged to."

"It belongs to one of Gracie's brothers-in-law. It's not that bad. Plus, I got a haircut and I shaved. And I'm not wearing a suit. I've decided that I don't care for them." She only stared at him. There was something else too, his tone. She didn't care for it one bit, and told him that. "I don't care. I like this new me. I've come to tell you a few things, then I'm going to leave you here."

"What are you talking about? I'm your wife. And you most certainly will not be leaving me here. What will people think when I return home and they find out what you've done to me?" He said that he was filing for divorce. "No you're not, William. You and I have three children now, and you'll not be leaving me alone to support them."

"They're not my children. And you're not pregnant. It took some digging, but I found out everything. Why are you still holding onto this lie? Is it so second nature to you that you don't even know how to tell the truth any longer?" She asked him what that was supposed to mean. "Just that. You have numerous affairs and as a result, you have two children that aren't mine. But it matters little. I'm going to try for full custody."

"No, I won't have it, William. *You* and I are perfect together. You said that yourself. It's why we married. *We* have two wonderful little boys and another one on the way. *We're* going to raise them as good men and *we're* going to be happy. I've told you this before, William." He said that he'd not been happy for some time, and that there wasn't a child. "I don't care about your happiness. You should be more concerned about mine. I'm going to have a baby."

"You say that a great deal. Like you're the only person in the world who has ever gotten knocked up. You're not, by the way. Pregnant, I mean. And I'm pretty sure that anyone that has had a baby didn't complain nearly as much as you do about it when you were. If you hated being pregnant so much, why did you not take precautions with the boys? I would have if I had been having affairs and bringing babies into the world that didn't belong to my husband." Cora told him he was missing the point. "No, I don't think I am. But that's not why I'm here. I'm here to tell you that I've taken control of my life, and that means that you're no longer a part of it."

"You cannot be serious. Did one of my family put you up to this? Did they tell you how horrible I am to them?" William told her that she was horrible to everyone. "I most certainly am not. I'm the only person that will tell it like it is and they hate that. Well, when I get out of here, don't think I won't have a few things to say to my sister and mother. They're going to be very sorry that—"

"Oh, they're very sorry." She told him good. "Not about you. Though, indirectly I guess. But they feel sorry for me. Did you know that when my check was deposited in the bank, you were to pay the bills with it? And the credit card payments? Not to mention, the car payment as well as anything else that we owe?"

"I was going to do that. I had it on my list for you to ask for a raise at work. You should, you know. You deserve it, and the extra income will get us back on track. I've told you before that you work too hard for the amount that you're paid." She smiled at him. "William, I just can't stand that you look like a hobo. Why are you wearing those pants? Can you imagine what our friends would say if they could see you now?"

"I like them. Gideon gave them to me. And this shirt belonged to one of his brothers. They're a wonderful family. And I'd be more concerned with what they're going to say about you being in jail, as well as lying about having a child. There is no baby, Cora. You can't have them. Why are you continuing with this charade? All this, this will certainly set your so-called friends on their ear." He laughed, but it was bitter and she didn't like it. "I'm filing for divorce and custody of the children. Both of them. Also, I'm suing you for leaving me bankrupt. As well as adultery and mental anguish, and a few other things that I can't think of right now. That's why I came by, to tell you that and to let you know that I should never have married you. But you did open my eyes to a great many things."

"Well, that's a good thing, then. Opening one's eyes is enough to keep us together. William, just get me out of here. Then we'll talk. I'll talk and you'll listen. We need to be together. It's not fair of you to listen to their side and not mine. And we both know that mine is much more important and sane than theirs will be." He said that it wasn't good things that he'd been opened to. "William, I just don't like you right now. I'd like for you to go away and come back when you're in a better frame of mind. And to be dressed properly. We'll work this out, we always do."

"No, we only work things out so that they're in your favor. I'm finished with that. Sadly, I should have seen that earlier, but I'm getting there now." He turned and started away when he stopped and looked at her. "You're a horrible person. Have been for years, but what you said to your sister…that, I think, is when I realized that I couldn't be a part of your life again. The things that she went through, you should have been there for her. Instead, you acted like she was better off without her family."

"What time are you talking about? And you know as well as I that Gracie could have done better." He told her what he was referring to. "So? The baby was better off dead than to be with them as parents. He was lazy, and my sister.... Well, Gracie is never going to amount to anything worthy. Not like us."

"You mean you." Cora didn't know what he was talking about and asked him. "You mean there isn't anyone out there that is up to your standards. The way that you think things should be done or said. I never realized it, but you're not even sorry that you're a fucking cunt, are you? I should have seen that years ago."

She was still standing there when her breakfast tray was brought to her. Cora took it without checking, and heard the laughter as the police woman walked away. She wondered if they had heard the exchange between her and William as she lifted the cover off her food.

"Damn it all to hell and back." There were scrambled eggs that looked like they'd been cooked over an open flame with bits of charred something was in them. Two limp pieces of bacon that looked like someone had taken a bite out of each one. A bagel with what appeared to be onions on it, as well as a cup of coffee that had three cubes of ice still floating in it.

Setting it on the floor without touching it, she thought about kicking it across the cell. But she had to think, and clearly. There were things afoot, as her friend used to say. And she had to get it together before it came back to bite her in the ass. If she didn't, breakfast was going to be the least of her worries.

~~~

"Her name is Delia. I don't believe she had a last name, but if she did, I've long since forgotten it." Gracie held the ice pack on her face as she sat there. Taking a tumble out of the bed when Gideon started thrashing was her fault, but the two

103

men were taking it very hard. Caroline smiled at her as she spoke. "Here, child. I can fix that."

The touch was gentle, and in seconds the pain was gone. Putting the pack down, Gracie looked around the room. There were more people in here than she'd ever seen anywhere, and all of them, even the dragons, were looking like they were ready for war.

"This person, she thought that she had a dragon, correct?" Caroline nodded at her. "Okay, I understand that. And even why she'd want one. But why now? I mean, Helena has been gone for a bit now, right?"

"Yes, one year tomorrow." She was sure that was supposed to mean something, but she didn't have any idea. "She'd need a dragon to bring her back from the dead. For what reason I don't know, but the heart of a dragon can do all sorts of things if you know how. I'm to understand that you've been gathering the books of past witches. Very good."

"They come to me and tell me where they are and I go get them. But that doesn't mean that I understand this. Yes, I believe there can be magical people—I'd have to be naïve not to know that—but why is it important to these witches that I have them?" Caroline sat down in front of her and took her hand. "You going to read my palm?"

"Sort of." Touching her fingers to the middle of her palm, she pulled a long line of something out of it. "This is the magic that makes you be able to see the dead. As you can see, it's white, which is good. And there, where it attaches to your hand, it's red. That's because it's at your heart."

"That makes a difference?" Caroline said that it did, for anyone to trust her. "Okay, so they can see this magic and that it's at my heart and it's white. But that doesn't explain to me why me."

"True. Let me ask you something. How many people do you think can see the dead? I don't mean people who profess it, but those that actually can see them?" Gracie said she didn't know. "Right, because there are only a handful of them. Two of which are in this room."

"You?" Caroline said no, it was Gobi. They all turned and stared at the other woman as she knitted. "Why didn't the witches go to her? Not that I mind helping them, but I need to understand this."

"Have you told anyone that once you touch the books, you know them? You might not understand them, but you do know them?" She felt her face heat up and Caroline laughed. "It's not a bad thing, my dear. You know as well as the rest of us that the books can only be opened by the blood of the queen. Her daughter. Do you know why?"

"No, but I'm sure you do." Caroline said it was because of her daughter. "Beth? I don't understand. She was just a baby when.... Please, she's not here is she?"

"No, child, she can't come to you. But when she died, with you wrapped around her, she told the dead that came to get her that you tried to save her. That you were special to her and would be to them as well." Gracie said she was her mother. "Yes, a loving wonderful mother who tried, even with her own body broken and nearly beyond repair, to save her."

She thought it would be what any parent would do, but then thought of her sister. Gracie had no idea if she would do that or not, but for some reason, Gracie thought Cora would always think of herself over others. No matter how they were related to her.

"So, you're saying that these witches come to me to help them because of what I did for my little girl." Caroline said that was some of it. "Then what's the rest? Something to do with.... It's the dragons, isn't it?"

"And the former king and queen of them. You see, they knew about you and that you'd come to their family." Gracie said that someone had said that. "Good, then you understand that they've had a hand in all their children's lives, well before they were born too."

"I've been picked to see the dead and carry out their wishes for them. And not only that, I can see what's in these locked books. Should I be afraid? I mean, to be honest, I'm slightly freaked out." Caroline laughed, but Gracie failed to see the humor in it. "This is very serious. And now we have this witch that is trying her best to raise another one to come after us."

"Yes, but she won't be able to do that." Gracie asked her why not. "Because Helena was killed by her own magic and left in water, below a mountain."

Something occurred to her. Gracie thought about where she'd seen it, or even had read about it, but when it occurred to her, she was no less skeptical. Caroline just smiled, as if she already understood her.

"The book that I gave Asher, the first one, it said that a body can't be raised from a watery grave. That the elements, this would include the mountain as well, that hold her there would have to agree to release her after the waterways have dried to nothing." Caroline nodded and Gobi came to join her. "And that the holder of the book would need to be willing to embrace the dead into their heart. I'm sure none of that is going to happen."

"Correct." Gracie looked over at Gideon, who was sitting to her left, Onimia to her right. "And while she knows that there are dragons here, more than likely from the troubled witches that we had here before, she knows not who they are or how many. All she is doing is guessing at this point."

"How do you know?" Caroline said because Delia invaded the wrong man and not the king as she had hoped, nor did she get the dragon. "I see. So, we should just not worry about her? I'd like that very much."

"Oh no, she must be killed. And you're going to do that." Gracie shook her head and stood up. So did Gobi and Caroline. "You have to, you see. It's you who she will come after if she finds out that you can speak to the dead. With you, she can get the other books."

"But why me? I mean, isn't that sort of like dangling me from the end of a hook in a pond of fish? I'm no more capable of keeping myself safe than I was at keeping myself out of trouble." Her mom laughed and Gracie smiled. "Mom, help me here. Tell her that I'm not good at death and such."

"Gracie, I hate to agree with Caroline, but you're a good deal stronger than you think you are, and would be perfect for the job if you needed to do it." Her mom smiled at her; it was soft and comforting, the kind that she had for her everyday she was in the hospital. "You have lost so much for someone so young. A husband that loved you dearly. A child...I cannot imagine what you feel losing your only child like that. But you've grown so much in the last few days, here with this family. And I think...no, I know that if anyone could do this, it would be you. Why, just look how you stood up to your sister. That took some guts. You should have done it years ago."

"I should have, but that doesn't mean I can kill someone." Her mom nodded. "Mom, she means for me to murder this woman."

"Yes, she does. Before she murders you, and I think that's

107

what you should focus on." Her ever practical mom. "Also, and this might just be me, but I think this witch is going to be in for a rude awakening if she messes with my little girl. You're scary when you're on a roll."

She'd never been on a roll in her life. And murdering someone, no matter the circumstances, wasn't a good way to start, she thought. But she would do what was necessary to keep the family safe. Both of them. Gracie had come to love the Bensons as much as she did her own.

As they planned and plotted, Gracie thought of her sister. Cora was in jail, but she wouldn't be there long. A couple of days at the most, Simeon had told her. Then she'd be free to terrorize people once again.

Connor, Cora's oldest, came and sat beside her. "My mother is a bad person." She asked him why he'd say that. "She says things bad about everybody. Except the men she has come and fix her room."

"I'm sorry. What?" He told her how her mom had people coming to the house to fix broken things in the bedroom. And that sometimes they'd stay all day when she promised them things. "Promised you things for what?"

"We were supposed to go to the pool one time, but the broken stuff took all day. She said it was a surprise for Dad, so if we didn't tell him, then we could go to the pool for the whole day the next afternoon. But we didn't go then because something else broke." Gracie wondered how many times a week her sister had broken things in her house. "And she don't like none of the ladies at the park. She said that they're.... Mother calls them bad names."

"She doesn't like. And that's not nice at all." Neither was having people in your bedroom with your kids down the hall. Looking around, she saw Sally and wondered what she'd say about all this. "I want you to do me a big favor, please?"

"Anything, Aunt Gracie. And so you know, me and Mike, we think you're the best in the world. Dad too. He's been hurting bad, huh?" She said that she thought that he was. "We'll hug him extra. Mother won't tell us to leave him alone."

Gracie was beginning to dislike her sister more and more. "I want you to first, hug your dad anytime you want. I mean, even if you want to get up out of your bed, go to his room, and hug him, you and Mike do it." He said that he could do that. "The favor. The favor I need for you to do for me is to have as much fun as possible. The Bensons are very nice people. And they love you guys already as much as I do."

"They said we can call them Grandma and Grandda." She knew that too. They'd asked if it would be all right with her mom. "And they have a swing that we can use when it gets warm again."

"Yes, I heard about that too." Asher had done that for Mark, and all the boys were getting along very well. "You need anything, you come and see either me or Gideon or Onimia, all right?"

"Yes. All right." He looked at the two men and then up at her. "You love them, huh? Both of them. They're really nice, and said I could call them uncle if me and Mike were gonna be hanging around."

"Yes, I think I do love them. Very much so." He sat with her for a little while longer. Mike and the others went to the entertainment room. Gracie wasn't sure what to do with the information that she'd gotten from Connor, but she had a feeling that William needed to know. But how did you tell a man that his wife had brought other men to his bed?

Chapter 8

The castle was nearly complete and only had a few minor kinks in the walls. Gideon had a feeling that it would right itself once it was complete. The turret that was to the right of the door was still being worked on, as well as some of the walls that butted against the mountain. He watched as the crew of faeries brought in another piece of furniture that had been completed earlier last week.

"Do you think that once we get it finished it'll have Wi-Fi as well as any other modern conveniences?" He nodded at Onimia as they pulled another long rug off the back of the truck. "Yeah, that's what I was thinking too. The kitchen is all but finished, did you see that?"

"Yes. I was down there yesterday, and the brownie in charge of the area said they were just waiting on the stock to come in. But that won't be for another month...about Christmas, I guess." He and Onimia took the carpet, a long runner for the main hallway, to where the tag on it had read. "I was wondering if your parents will be around when it's done. I mean, they are the ones that gave us everything we

111

needed to start this thing."

"Dad isn't keen on going into it until it's complete. Mom said he might not even then." Gideon hadn't thought of that. He had died in the place. "Did you see the sword that Peck found for Mark? It's beautiful and magical."

"I saw it. That was really great that he did that for him. I think the kid was feeling a little too old for the girls. He's sure having a good time with Connor and Mike." Onimia said he was as well. "William. That poor guy. He's really had his feet swept out from under him."

"Gracie wants to go and see her sometime soon. Are you going with her?" He said that he was and asked if he was too. "No. I want to but I have something to do today with Sally. She and I are going to go to the mushroom patch and put mulch on it. She said by spring, she wants it ready to go."

"You're going to keep her safe." He said it was his day, and he was actually looking forward to it. "I'm glad you'll be with her. And make sure that she enlarges the patch. She'd been talking about doing that for years before she got sick."

They didn't talk about the fact that she had died, nor about their dad having died. They were there now, and that was what was important. Gideon picked up the next box and read the label. They were to take this one to the kitchen.

Entering the big room, he paused in the entrance way. Gracie was there, along with two of the women from town that had been hired to come and cook for the castle. There wouldn't be much, not lavish groups of people or even much more than family, but they were a big lot and they'd decided that two cooks would be good so that they could meet for dinner a few times a week. But to him it looked like things weren't going well.

"I have no idea. All I know is what I've been told, and that is for you to get your herbs from the drying house rather than anything you might bring from the outside." The woman crossed her arms over her bosom and said she only worked with fresh things. "Be that as it may, you will use the things that are grown in the gardens here and not anything that is brought in. And when there are things brought in, the king or queen will look it over."

"So they'll inspect everything that I cook. Will they have a taster as well? Perhaps someone to die in place of them?" The woman huffed, taking off her apron. "I cannot be expected to work like this. I have to have things just the way that I like them and no other way. If I must do this, then you'll not have my cooking. What do you say to that?"

"Goodbye." The woman looked at the other one and then back at Gracie. "I'm sure that you'll understand that we'll only pay you for the time you worked here and nothing more. It's too bad that you couldn't abide by the rules that you agreed to when you signed—"

"Now that's not right." Gracie asked the woman why not, she'd not worked. "No, I mean, you are to compromise with me. Tell me that I can do this small thing, and I'll perhaps have to work out something to give back to you. We are negotiating."

"No, I'm telling you that your services are no longer needed. I'm sure that you know the way out." Gracie turned her back on the woman and saw him. "In fact, I'm sure that Gideon, the brother to the king, can show you the doorway out. Gideon, love, please make sure that Ms. Jenkins makes it out to her car without any issues."

Setting the box on the table, he was hard pressed not to laugh at the expression on Ms. Jenkins' face. He was sure that she'd thought Gracie was going to give in. And when she

113

didn't, things didn't go the way she had hoped. As he guided her to the door, he wondered why Gracie would be so hard on the woman.

Her sister is here. He asked Gracie if it was the other woman. *No. Her dead sister is here. She told me that her plan is to poison the kingdom. That her herbs are laced with an iron additive that would make them ill, or cause their death should they not have the magic to counter that.*

So, her plan to bring in her own herbs, that's how she was planning to do it? Why? What did we do to her? Gracie laughed. *Oh, this is going to be good, no doubt. What does she have in her head that we did?*

You didn't hire her son-in-law to help out at the castle. Having all the work done from outside contractors, which is how she thinks you did this, is wrong for the community. By the way, she has no support in this with the community. It's all about her deadbeat son-in-law. She was hoping that he'd get a job and stop sponging off her by taking his equally lazy wife, her daughter, someplace else. Gideon walked Ms. Jenkins to her car, saying nothing to her. As he watched her drive away, Gracie spoke to him again. *Do you think that Essie is going to be mad at me for firing that woman?*

No. Christ, no. You probably saved that woman's life by you doing it. Had Essie or one of the other women been involved, I'm sure the outcome would have been vastly different. She said thanks but didn't sound so sure. *The truck is empty and we're waiting on another load. Do you have some time that I could show you how much I appreciate you?*

You mean sex? He laughed and said that was it exactly. *You're like a kid with a new toy, did you know that? I mean, I'm having a blast, but there is such a thing as moderation.*

Not with you, there's not. He felt her need like a slap in the face. *Where are you? Still in the kitchen? If so, there is a large*

114

pantry close by that —

I'm near the herb garden. Good, he thought, outside. *Meet me at the forest line, where the path is to the outside entrance.*

He was nearly at a run when he was close. Gideon wanted her so badly that before he touched her, he knew that he needed to come first. It was that, or rut her like a boar...though that did have some appeal to it. All thoughts of coming first flew out the window when he saw her naked leaning against the tree.

"Christ, you're beautiful." Nodding, she told him to hurry. "I'm not going to go easy. I can never go easy where you're concerned. Bend over."

When she did as he asked quickly, he came up behind her and slammed his cock home. Taking her hard, hearing her breathless need, her heart pounding as hard as his, he leaned over her and bit into her shoulder. Gracie came apart, her body and her mouth screaming out a release that tightened around his cock so tightly that he could barely move. And when he came, Gideon wasn't sure if he'd ever be the same.

But he wasn't finished. His need seemed to spike higher, his cock hurt to release inside of her again. As he fucked her, holding her body to his tightly, he watched her breasts move, her lips tighten. And when a thought, just an image of her taking him into his mouth, entered his head, he cried out his second release as he raked his nails down her back, drawing blood.

Gideon couldn't move. He was sure that as soon as he let her go, he was going to fall on his ass and humiliate himself. That or take a nap, for about a week. When she stood up in front of him, he held her tightly. Gracie laughed when he told her not to move yet.

"I think you broke me." Gracie turned her head and

115

kissed him on the nose. "No, I'm serious. I cannot move any more today. So when the next truck gets here, you'll have to unload it yourself."

"I might." Gracie turned in his arms, and Gideon told her how much he loved her. "And I you. I didn't think that was going to be possible, but I do love you."

They dressed after that. He told her that she could with just a thought, but she said that was a little too freaky for her at the moment. When she sat on the ground, leaning against the tree, he asked her if she was all right. At her nod, he sat down beside her.

"What time did you want to leave in the morning? Or have you decided to go see Cora later?" Gracie didn't answer him so he changed the subject. "William is doing a great job working with Asher. He's a whiz at the computer, and is going to set up the monitoring system at the castle when they're ready to move in."

"He told me this morning that he was fired from his job. I guess that Cora made some purchases on his company credit card that they didn't care for. Apparently, it's not the first time." Gideon knew that too. "They've lost their house as well. The contents are going to be sold at an auction to the highest bidder. I'm going to go there with him to see if we can get some of his things. Oh, and I've made arrangements to have the boys and him get some clothing. All they have is what they brought here."

"William is taking this much better than anyone I know. I think that this has been coming on for a long time. But the worst part is, she's hurt her kids in this." She told him what Connor had told her about the men fixing things in the bedroom. "What a bitch. I'm sorry, I know that she's your sister, but she is not a good person."

"No, she's not. As for tomorrow. I think I'd rather see her alone. I know that it's ill-advised for me to see her at all — it will do me little good — but I want to hear what she has to say about this. Especially about the kids and having men there." He said he understood, but he'd still like to be there for her when she was finished. "I'd like that as well. I don't know that she'll be her usual self, but I can almost bet on it."

As they made arrangements about tomorrow, they made their way back to the castle. There were two more trucks there now, and Gracie helped them unload the boxes. When she and Onimia wandered off a few minutes later, he smiled. Gideon hoped he was just as exhausted when she finished with him.

~~~

Delia looked over the map that had been crudely drawn. The castle was there, she could see it, but as far as the tree line and its nearness to it, she was sure that it was off. The castle, now in ruins, was never that large. She looked around when she felt someone joining her in the little den she'd taken for herself.

The cave, or just the mouth of it, looked like any other cave that dotted the hills surrounding the keep of the castle. She knew that she'd have to stay away from the area, at least until she had what she wanted. The dragon, the last one, would be her greatest catch. Looking at the map that had been sent to her from Helenia, Delia wondered what she'd said in the lettering that was with it.

She knew Helena couldn't read. Delia could barely write her own name, much less read the words that had been scratched on the paper. She needed to hire someone to do such things, but she feared, like most witches, that someone smarter than her would take her magic. Which, to Delia's way of thinking, could be most any idiot on the roads now a days.

But she also knew that she was smarter than the average witch.

"I'm still here, am I not?" Looking around her rooms, she was satisfied that she'd used a bit more magic than necessary to make this place livable. There was a great bed with silken sheets upon it. Pillows were all over the floor around it as well as the thick mattress. Delia had gotten used to the finer things that life had to offer her, and she wasn't one to skimp for her own comfort. "There is always someone around that I can steal from should I need a bit more."

She still needed to get the dragon to raise the dead witch so that she could get her books. Helena had kept the best books when it came to potions and spells. While her magic was mediocre at best, Delia was sure that she could and would improve upon it.

The drawing of a dragon was on the map that she'd been sent. A fucking dragon. There were other creatures as well, though not anything she could make out—the tiny winged things might be faeries—but a dragon was the best thing she'd heard in a very long time.

Delia looked up when she heard a twig break not far from the mouth of her home. Two people, a man and a woman, were coming a little closer than she wanted. But before she could send them on their way with a bit of magic, they embraced, kissing passionately while Delia watched them.

They were unaware of her, so she moved out of the mouth of the cave a little. To see them, to watch them take each other with such passion, stirred something she'd thought long dead inside of her. As they stripped off their clothing, hands were touching each other with such need that she felt her own rise up.

The man was the aggressor. Delia thought of the sex she

could have with this man, how she would make him her slave. And when he pulled from the woman, she saw his cock. Christ, he was huge, and the thought of it made her hand slide down to her own pussy to think of the way that he'd stretch her.

The woman was loud in her passion, the man demanding in his needs. He ate the woman with such vigor, like she was a feast that only he could have. As she came, screaming to the man to make her come again, Delia's fingers danced inside of her and wished that the man would do the same for her. His name was Onimia, a name she knew that she'd be crying out nightly for the next month or so as she pleasured herself.

Delia cried out when the man did, her body giving her the most incredible pleasure as he came all over the woman beneath him. When he stood up, his cock in his hand, Delia wanted to go and take him into her mouth, a thing that she'd never enjoyed before but thought she might with him. When he came again, spraying his seed upon the woman, she cried out again, careful to keep her voice down as low as she could.

When they kissed again, she staggered into the cave. She'd had sex before over the years, but that had been the best she'd ever enjoyed. Christ, to have a man like him between her thighs might be worth having to have sex with a human. And his cock? Well, she was sure that it would taste as delicious as it looked. Perhaps more so.

Falling into her bed, she closed her eyes while her body, still racked with spasms of her release, shook her muscles. Delia smiled; she was feeling sated as well as relaxed. More so than she had in decades. Sex. Who would have thought that it could be such a wonderful sleep drug?

When she woke, the cave was dark. Spreading her hands wide the room brightened momentarily before becoming darker than before. There wasn't even a bit of moonlight to break the inky darkness around her. Trying once again, she froze in mid conjure when she heard the laughter.

"Who goes there? I am the great witch Delia. You must know that I shall kill you if you try and harm me." The laughter again, and this time it seemed closer. "What are you doing here?"

"I live here." The snap of light was blinding for a moment, but when her eyes adjusted to it, she wished for darkness again. "Ah, so you know who I am. I'm always surprised by that. I mean, to me, I'm just a witch. But I guess being what I am to a great many people gives me a certain aura, don't you think?"

"Ariannona. We thought you long dead." The witch stood up and moved around the room. "Have you come here for a reason? But I wish to welcome you. I should have done so first. What have you been doing for yourself? You look better than I thought you might."

"You thought me dead, so that's not telling me overly much, now is it? And you're no more welcoming me here than I wish to be here with you, Delia. What is it you hope to find, being so close to the grounds where the castle is? Money? There is none for you. Witchcraft? Again, nothing for you there either. What do you want?" She couldn't think beyond her fear of this woman. "Shall I find out for myself?"

The raping of her mind was quick, but no less painful for it. As she rubbed a hanky to her nose to stop the bleeding, Delia tried to think what she could do now. Ariannona was a strong and very old witch. Twice her age, with more powers than ten of her kind.

"Ah, so you've had a little entertainment, have you? Not very nice of you to spy on people when they're having a bit of fun. But then, you never were one to be nice, were you? And if you think to raise Helena, there is something else you should know. She's not just dead, but beyond your ability to bring to life again." She asked her why, forgetting her fear for a moment. "She is in the belly of a mountain, covered in water, with a magical spell to hold her there. I'm afraid you're shit out of luck if you think you're going to convince anyone to let her out."

"Why was I not told this?" Ariannona just cocked a brow at her. "My lady, why is this not common knowledge? I would not have traveled so far to—"

"Cut the bullshit. You were going to raise her up only to murder her again when she gave up the whereabouts of her book. Which, by the way, is in a safe place. The king of dragons has it. All of them, as a matter of fact." Ariannona traveled around the room, touching Delia's things as if she were in a market deciding on what she wanted. "You have a lot of nice things here. Why, I can't figure out, but they are nice. Too bad you're going to have to leave them behind."

"Why would I do that?" Caroline appeared in the room with them, as did Lelani and a witch she did not know. "This is unfair. You know that, do you not? If your plan is to bring me to justice, then I am to get fair warning."

"Sure, if we thought about bringing you to justice. We are, but not before the council. I'm going to make my own sort of justice concerning you." Delia felt her skin tighten and her body ready to run. She didn't have anywhere to go, but she would run if the chance came to her. "Delia, you do know that we're well within our rights to kill you because of the plan you had to raise the dead. That, so you know, is a no-no."

"I wish to be brought before the counsel." She wasn't sure that she should do that either, but Delia had a feeling that she might suffer less if she were. Just the thing she'd done to one of these women would be enough for them to burn her. "I am evoking my rights, as a witch, to be brought up on charges before the Witches Counsel."

"Too fucking bad." She felt the tightening of the rope as it curled around her throat. And before she could do much more than claw at it, the woman from earlier, the one having sex at her front door, stood in the room as well.

There was something about her, something that she hadn't noticed before. Magic, a great deal of it, surrounded her. As she stood there, staring at her, Delia felt the coil of the rope lessen from around her.

"You've come here to kill my mate." Delia denied it, told her that she only wanted a dragon. "Yes, my mate."

The dragon, a great beast of a thing, appeared in the room with them. Then another, and another. Soon there were half a dozen of them, the colors on them so rich, their scales, a fortune worth of them, sparkling their beauty all around the room. What she could do with so many made her senseless with greed.

"We could make so much, and the wealth would be nothing compared to what we'd have in admiration from others. They would bow before me. Tell me what a great witch I am with so many. Thank you so much for bringing them to me." The woman looked at the dragons, then at her. "I will share my wealth with you, my dear."

"No, you won't." The lashing of the magic took her breath away. Had she been standing, she was sure that it would have put her to the ground. The second time it hit her, she felt her head split, and her back breaking under it. She was going to be killed and not tell the world of her find.

"Delia, can you hear me?" She had to work hard to focus

on the woman standing before her. She looked familiar, but was not one that she could place at the moment, not with the pain in her head. "'Tis your sister, Janie."

"Janie? But you're dead. These people, they have risen you? Without my permission?" She said they had not. "Then you are not to be here. Begone with you."

"Nay, I will not. I have come to avenge my death. You see the woman there, the one that has killed you? She is a death watcher. A death watcher after all this time. I went to her and told her what you had done, the people — not all witches — that you've killed. I've been watching you, sister dear, and the list I have is longer than your reach to kill anyone else."

This time the lash of magic was welcomed. It stopped the pain that made it hard for her to breathe, stopped her head from pounding as if someone had put a pike deep within her. As the warmth of her blood spilled from her body, she looked at her sister as she laughed. She'd get her, she thought, as soon as she crossed over.

Then the words, those simple words that no witch wanted to hear, not even in jest, were spoken. And by the great Ariannona, white witch to the king and queen of dragons.

"I condemn you to reside forevermore in the earth of this mountain. Water shall be your blood. Dirt your air. Forevermore and a day, Delia, witch of no consequence. You will never rise without the permission of the King of Dragons."

No, her mind screamed as she felt the earth close in around her. Then the water, filling her body so that no one, not even her long dead sister, could bring her back if she'd had a mind to.

Chapter 9

Cora hated the jumpsuit that she'd been given. Up until today she'd been wearing her own things. Of course they were dirty beyond anything that she'd ever wear again, but she had a visitor, and she hoped that once she talked to William things would be over. This was senseless. She'd been in here for six days now, and that was more than long enough for him to get whatever it was out of his system. When her sister sat across form her, she asked where her husband was.

"My husband? He's out in the lobby. Why would you care to see him?" She told Gracie she meant her husband. "Oh, Bill, which is what he wants to be called from now on, in case you're interested, is at work. Doing a good job of it too. You should—"

"His name is William, and I'd thank you to remember that. But he's gone home? Without me?" Gracie shook her head. "Then I don't understand. He can't work from home, I won't have it. What are you talking about?"

"He's working for Asher, my brother-in-law. And as I was saying, he's doing a fine job too. Why just yesterday he—"

125

"Gracie, I don't care. Why are you here instead of him?" Gracie smiled but said nothing. "And my sons, where are they? I'd like to see them. I've so missed them."

"Funny, they don't miss you at all. And they're having a good time too. Connor had to have stiches yesterday, but he loved it." Cora asked her what she'd done to him. "Only you would think to say that. Not 'is he all right?' or 'does he need anything?' I did nothing to him. He fell out of a tree he was climbing with Mark."

"I do not allow them to climb trees. That's just ridiculous. What really happened?" Gracie looked at the guard that was in the room with them, and when he nodded, Gracie pulled out her phone. After Cora was warned not to touch it, Gracie showed her pictures of her children, and the long gash that was on Connor's leg. "You did this to them. By letting them be hooligans. I swear to you, Gracie, there are days when I think you might have been better off with your child dying. I know that I've told you this before, but you aren't fit to have a child. You're very lucky in that. Can you imagine what sort of mangled mess she'd be in by now?"

"She was a mangled mess, Cora. Her little body was broken nearly in half when the car seat that she was in hit the pole as she flew through the air. But you'd not know that, would you? Seeing as how you refused to go to the funeral since she was dead and would not care if you were there. Had to get your nails done, I heard." Cora told her it was a standing appointment. "Yes, so I was told."

"Are we going to bring this up again? My God, Gracie, you act as if you're the only one that has ever lost a child. It happens, get over it. Christ, I've lost my credit cards and didn't whine as much as you do about a child that was too small to matter to anyone." Gracie told her that she mattered

126

to her. "Yes, and it's been three years, it's time to move on."

Gracie put her phone away and Cora started to tell her to bring it out again. She wondered if she could get prints made of some of the shots of her boys. To have them framed and hanging in her cell would be a lot nicer than looking at the gray walls. Gracie pulled out a notebook, after gaining permission again.

"Gracie, you do not have to ask them permission for every little thing you do. It's not like I'm going to be here much longer. Which reminds me, where is William in getting me set free? I'm sure by now I've paid for hitting that person." Gracie opened the notebook, and Cora started to reach for it when she was slapped on her hand by her sister. "That was uncalled for. I only wanted to hurry this...whatever it is so that you can get to the point of you being here."

"One, Bill isn't working to get you out of jail. To be honest with you, I think he likes you being here. Two, there is no home for you to go to even if you were to leave this place. The office where Bill worked has taken it, and all the furniture and things in it, to be auctioned to pay bills. Three, you have been—"

"Wait a minute, they can't take my home. I have worked hard to make that look good. And what will my neighbors think? Oh Gracie, tell me that it's not been put in the paper about this. I'll never be able to show my face at the country club again. Christ, this is a royal fuck up. I'll have to have a party, to assure the girls I play tennis with that...." Gracie was staring at her. "What is it now? You're pissed because my friends will wonder what happened to me?"

"No. Did you think of the effect this might have on your kids? What they might be thinking about this? They're losing their home, their toys and clothing, and all you can think about is how this will make you look." Cora told her looks were everything in her social group. "I'm sure that I wouldn't know."

"Gracie, I expect you to help me out of this mess. You told me you have money, though I still find that hard to believe. You go to the auction and get my things back. I'll make sure you have a list of things that I simply can't live without. This might be a good thing, you know. William and I can start fresh. Maybe you should just help us get a bigger better home." Cora was thinking of all the things her sister could do for her. "I'm supposing that they took the cars too. Well, no matter. I'll add that to the list."

"I'm not going to help you buy anything, and I can't believe you'd think I would." Cora asked her why not. "Well, for one thing, you're a bitch. And secondly, I've decided that I don't much care for you."

"Well, that's fine. I don't care for you either. But you will help me, Gracie. I'm going to have a baby, and I can't have it and be out on the streets with my family." Gracie picked up her notebook again. "I'm glad that's settled."

"You have a court appearance on Friday. You'll be brought some clothing to wear to it, but nothing else." Cora asked what that was about. "The company that Bill used to work for is demanding that you pay them back for the purchases that you made on his company credit card, that will be above what they think will be coming in from the auction."

"Add that to the list of things you can take care of. What else?" Gracie looked at her notes, but not before Cora saw the tears. "Don't be upset for me. I'll come out on top of this. I always do. Now, what else?"

"I'm not concerned for your welfare at all, Cora, and I won't be again." She put the notebook away without making notes on things. "I came here with the hope that we could have a talk, that the two of us could at least iron out some things. But you'll never change. Will you?"

"Change into what? Someone like you? Someone that lazes about the house moping about a long dead husband? I told you he was worthless, and that just proves it. I don't need to change, I like me just the way I am." Gracie stood up, and Cora was stuck to the seat by a handcuff. "Gracie, when am I getting out of here? And when is William bringing the boys by to see me?"

"He's filed for divorce. And with my connections, he's going to get it." She asked her sister why she'd do such a fool thing. "Because he's a good man that you hurt. And after tomorrow, I'm betting that you might be in here a good deal longer than you want. I wonder how you're going to get your jollies while here in prison. And so you know, everything that I've told you? Yes, it's in your local paper too. I did that for you."

Cora was taken back to her cell after Gracie left. She had no doubts that she'd be out in the morning, if not later today. There wasn't any way Gracie would be able to leave her here, not with her having a baby. And they were sisters.

To have Gracie paying off all her debt was a stroke of genius, she thought. It hadn't occurred to her, because she had no idea her sister had money, to tell her to do it before now. Christ, to have a nicer home? That would have all her friends so jealous. Then she thought of the company taking her home.

"I'll blame it all on William. He'll be a big man and say that he was gambling with the money or something. That we're going to get him help." She liked that too. It would give her some much needed sympathy from them.

The longer she sat there, planning out her new life, the more excited she got. Cora knew that Gracie might not do any of this for her, but she would for the boys. She was very affectionate to them, and Cora decided to use them to get what she wanted. Maybe even play the pregnancy card again. Putting her hand over the small bump, she smirked. Perhaps there was or wasn't a baby, but if she believed it, then it would be fact. She had read about this sort of thing before. Things were about to get very nice for her and her little family.

By the time her dinner came, she was well into how to get a built home from her sister, rather than take someone else's cast off. She'd never had a brand new house before, one where she got to pick out everything. Of course, the house that she and William had had been new, but it was finished by the time she'd convinced him that they needed it, and nothing was really hers. This time would be perfect.

When her dinner tray was brought, she was handed a thick envelope. Before she could ask what it was, the man standing there, one she didn't know, told her she'd been served. Then he laughed.

"Easiest one I've ever done. You can't run off when you see me coming." She asked him what the meaning of this was. "Read it. Not my job. I just make sure you got it. Don't even need you to sign for it, the cops will verify that you got it. You have a good day, Mrs. Daniels. I'm sure gonna."

Opening the envelope, she could only stare at the paperwork inside. She was being sued. Not just by the company that William worked for, but by him, as well as a list of people that she used. Her hairdresser. There was her manicurist, and even her housekeeper. They were all taking a bite out of her good mood. Gracie was going to have a lot to help her with now. Laughing, she put the envelope under her pillow and laid down. Tomorrow was going to be a better day.

~~~

Gideon moved the last of the boxes from the truck. It was harder work, he thought, moving things into the castle than it had been to put up the walls. By the looks of it, he thought that last of the turrets would be done by the end of the week.

Simeon said his name and he hugged his brother to him. "I'm terrified." He asked him of what as he looked around. "Of knowing the unknown. You know that I'm the only one left."

It took him several seconds to realize what he was talking about, then he laughed. Simeon said he didn't think that it was the least bit funny. Gideon, of course, laughed harder.

"Don't you want to be happier than you've ever been, Simeon? Have a mate that is there for you for everything? They're pretty special, let me tell you." Simeon said he didn't care to have a mate, they were all sappy enough. "True, we are. But we're happy."

"I would rather be unhappy than to be walking around with this stupid grin on my face like you guys are all the time. Besides, Akassa and I have everything just the way we want it, and a mate wants things her way." He asked where he'd come up with that. "You guys. All you do is go around doing things that your mates want. What if I wanted something? Who is going to give it to me?"

Akassa asked what he was talking about. Gideon told the dragon, in detail, what Simeon had said. From the look on the other man's face, he'd bet that he had no idea that Simeon felt that way.

"Are you nuts? I want a mate now more than I want anything. Christ, have you seen the way they treat your

131

brothers? It's like they're gods." Gideon wasn't sure of all that. Just this morning Gracie had ripped him a new ass when he didn't put his dishes in the dishwasher. She was nervous, he got that, but gods? Not really.

"She's going to want to take over our lives." Akassa said that was fine with him. "I'm surprised that any of the others can make a move without asking for permission from their mates."

"You sound like a ten-year-old that needs a nap. Maybe you should take one. Or I can tell Mom what you're saying." Simeon begged him not to. "Then straighten your ass up and be happy someone out there wants to be a part of your life. You have no idea how much you'll love this woman when she gets here, nor how much you'll be willing to do for her to see her smile. Or to laugh. I swear—"

Come to the patch. Dropping the box on the ground, he headed to the mushroom patch where Onimia and his mom were. Shouting to the others to follow, he wished that he could ride rather than run. *We have company. I've sent the others to the skies.*

He was afraid for his mom. And just as he was letting his imagination run wild, he saw his dad and Asher pass him in the Jeep. Jumping in the back, he wasn't surprised to see Jed and Shane there as well. They were all going to help, no matter what it was.

Gideon wasn't sure what to expect, but seeing the women with his mom wasn't nearly as calming as it should have been. She was sitting on the ground, a blanket wrapped around her legs when they pulled up. Dad was the first to get to her. He dropped to his knees as soon as he touched her.

"I'm fine. It's those people that I'm concerned about." He didn't see anyone and asked his mom where. "Just beyond...I think they're hiding. Call the dragons in. And I'm betting they come back. I've only been hurt because they scared me a wee bit."

She lifted the blanket and he could see the gash in her leg. It made his belly churn a bit to see her bleeding so badly, but Lelani touched it with her fingers and the wound closed up. Mom thanked her and started to stand up.

"Just a minute more, if you please. I was...I thought that I was...I can't lose you again, lady love. I just can't." Dad sobbed a little as he held onto Mom. She was all right, but what of the visitors?

"Look, over there." Gideon looked where Keion was pointing. "Where do you suppose they all came from?"

He didn't know but they were armed, and not with guns, though that would have been scarier still, but with pitchforks and hammers. It also looked as if a few people had picked up whatever was in their yard as they left to come here.

"They're dead." Gideon glanced at Anthony when he spoke, then back at the crowd. "They're the people that were killed the night I was. I wonder how long they've been hanging around here."

"You mean, they're not going to hurt anyone?" Anthony said he wasn't sure about that, but they were here for something. "I don't understand. I mean, I know that we can see them, but how can the rest of them too?"

"Because they're giving off a great deal of magic, as a whole." Gideon went to stand next to Gracie when she spoke, quietly again. "And as for what they're here for, they don't even know. I believe they're dressed and carrying the same items that they had in their hands when they met their deaths. Most of them, I believe, were killed by someone they knew."

"They more than likely were. It was horrible that night.

Eve and I had just gone out to survey the damage when we could see it was about to begin. We knew, you see, that this was going to be the end for us." Everyone turned to look at the former king. "The storm was magical, made by Helena, and then the townspeople, on edge because of the damage made, were stirred up by her as well."

"Why didn't you try and stop her? Use your own magic to quell the people?" Anthony turned to him with a sad smile. "Or at the very least, ran and waited for things to cool down."

"My children. It would have meant their certain death. While we could not interfere with the events that were in motion, we could touch the lives of others, keeping them out of harm's way and put into a position to help them." Gideon asked if that wasn't the same thing, interfering. "Nay, not interfering with the events that were set for, but changing the lives of others, ones not involved in the event that happened to bring things to that point. I could not kill Helena, though I wished to. Her part, the making of the storm, would have happened anyway. Someone else would have stirred them up. Someone would have come along and killed us for a reason only they understood. But we knew her course and her actions. Following the timeline that brought us to today, this very time in your lives, we knew that people had to be put in place to help you. The wives of you all. The death of a few. It was necessary, you see, to keep you all safe."

"So these people, they're here for what reason?" Anthony grinned at Gracie. "I'm not sure that I like that look. Like I should know and you're waiting for me to get it."

"You do know. And you've already gotten it." She looked at him, then at the people standing there, looking lost and out of place. "Well?"

"They don't know that they're dead. And the few that

do, they've no idea what to do now." He nodded. "I have to somehow...we have to help them understand that there is nothing here for them."

"Yes, that's it." Anthony started to fade. "My time here is declining. I will return again, but for now, I must rest. It's difficult for me to appear to you like this."

When he was gone, Gideon waited. There really weren't any rules for this, he thought. Winging it, or whatever it was called, was all they had. Moving with Onimia and Gracie to the group of people, he noticed that some of them were fading while others were as solid looking as they were. He asked her about it.

"I don't fucking know." He almost laughed, but was afraid she'd hit him. She was tense, and teasing her brought out her temper. Maybe later he'd do it when she was tense again, but when they were alone. In case she got the upper hand. "I guess we just talk to them. Find out what they know, or even want for that matter."

The group didn't put down their arms, but they didn't appear to look like they wanted to hit them any longer. The man in front carried a pitchfork in his hands, but he looked like he hadn't any idea why he had it. He seemed to be the spokesman for the group.

"There was a storm." Gracie nodded and smiled. "There be something not right. You, you look strange to me. Why are you dressed so?"

"Do you know where you are?" He nodded, then shook his head. "Why are you armed, do you know that?"

"I was told that.... Someone told me.... Nay, I cannot say why I'm armed. Am I armed or feeding the stock?" She said she thought him to be armed. "I'm remembering. The black witch, she said that the king and queen, they did this to us."

135

"Did what? Made a storm? Does that really sound like something that they'd do?" A dragon landed softly on the ground in front of him and to Gracie's right. The man only glanced at it before shaking his head. "And Helena, we know it was her. What did she tell you they did?"

"It seemed right this morning, her telling us that the two of them killed the land and took away our crops. But now I'm thinking that a dragon would have just blown the flames of their belly at us, and not near drowned us with a storm." Gracie told him that was smart of him. "My family, do you know what has happened to them?"

"I don't, I'm sorry. But it has been a great many centuries since you drew up your arms against the king." He nodded, looking shamefaced. "What is your name, sir?"

"I'm not a sir, just Don. I'm pigmaster to the castle." Gracie nodded. "I've been dead a long time too; have I not, miss?"

"You have. As has the king and queen. These men, they're sons of the king and his mate. This is Onimia, fourth son to King Anthony and Queen Eve. The dragon here, his name is Akassa, last son to them." He bowed before them and looked at the rest of the family. "Don, I have a favor to ask of you. It's a huge one, but I should like to put a marker up for the names of the people that lost their lives that fateful day."

"There were a great many of us, miss. We did not have our mind in the right place. Do you think it would have been magic?" She said she was sure of it. "I thank you for your faith in me and mine. What is it you need for this marker?"

"Names. All the names that you can think of, as well as what they did for the castle when it was up and running." He smiled at her, his grin looking out of place knowing that he was gone. "You will come to me tonight, when the moon is full, and we'll start a list of them. And once we have all of them, even the small children, we'll work on getting something put up in their honor. No man, woman, or child should go unnoticed simply because some witch decided to hurt your king and queen."

When Don walked away, the pitchfork still in his hand but not at the ready, Gideon looked at Gracie. He was proud of her. She'd taken a situation that might have gone badly and made it right. And not only that, she'd given honor to those that had come to them. As they made their way to the house, Onimia telling the rest of the family what had happened, Gideon took her hand in his. He was truly in love with his mate.

Chapter 10

Gracie sat with her mom in the courtroom. She had had a long talk with her and then with Bill about today, and Bill had opted to stay at home with the boys. Gracie had been surprised that neither of them wanted to come and see their mom, and Bill was all right with that too. Tomorrow they were moving into their new home, and all of them were very excited about that.

When they were told to rise, they did so and watched when Cora was brought out. There was no money for an attorney for her. Gracie had offered to pay, but Bill said that she would just complain about him or find him lacking if she did that. Which, she supposed, was true. So Cora had a court appointed one, and she'd just have to take what happened to her.

Almost as soon as they were all seated, Cora jumped up from her seat and asked to speak to the judge. She said it was a private matter and that it should be handled in his chambers.

"Mrs. Daniels, this is a hearing to see what sort of punishment you should be given for your crimes." She said that she'd only slapped someone and that she was sorry. "Be that as it may, that isn't the only thing we're here to decide. There is the matter of your using your husband's company credit card, as well as a few other items that needs to be addressed."

"My goodness, that is old news. So what? I used the card. I wouldn't have had to if he hadn't cut me off from the ones that I was just as happy using." The judge, Judge Brown, asked her if she knew that the card was to be used for company related things. "Sure, but who cares? I mean, seriously, it happens all the time. If they want their money back, then they can take it from William's check until it's paid."

"I'm afraid it's a bit late for that." Cora was told to have a seat. She asked again if she could have a word with him. "No. This is a court of law, not some luncheon that you and I are having. You will have a seat and be quiet or I'll have to have you taken away."

"Your Honor, I'm a very well-known and well-loved person, and if this gets out that I'm in this unimportant jail, my friends will never let me live this down. They can be a bit cruel when they find someone is less than them. I mean, I'd do the same, but this is me. Why can't we just do this in private, get it over with, and I can go home?" He told her again to sit down. "You're not listening to me. I don't want to do this in public. You will either tell these others to get out or we'll conduct this business in your office. I would like to go back to my home. After I straighten out things with my mother and sister."

The judge looked in their direction, and she felt her face heat up when he smiled. Gracie wasn't sure if he was feeling sorry for her or humoring her sister. Either way, this wasn't going to go well for Cora. She was pissing the wrong people off. Again.

Her mom beamed, something that she'd been sharing a great deal lately. Happiness exuded from her every pore, it seemed, and this, Cora being put in her place, was making her extremely happy. It was her as well, but she was also very hurt by Cora's actions.

The judge looked back at Cora, seemingly having gotten permission to be unkind to her. "Mrs. Daniels, I don't give a good damn about your friends or lack of them. I don't care if you get embarrassed or if they find out about your bad behavior. But what I do care about, and you should as well, is whether or not you are going to sit down and shut up until someone asks you a direct question." Cora opened her mouth and the judge cut her off. "One word from you right now and I will put you back in your cell and have these proceedings without you. And that will not bode well for you at all."

The room laughed, but quietly, like they were afraid of him turning his wrath on them. The bailiff stood up, his smiled winning as he read off the charges against Cora. The slap was last, the other charges against her holding much more weight than it. Her sister was facing real jail time if something didn't go her way.

The proceedings were started just as Gideon and Onimia joined them. They were both dressed in expensive looking suits, and when Sally and Jacob joined them, it looked, to everyone in the room, as if they were there in support of Cora. When in fact, Gracie thought they all wanted her behind bars for a little while longer, if not forever.

The first person to be called up was the owner of the company that William had worked for. He was stiff and seemed to want to be anywhere but here. When he gave his statement, telling everyone that Mrs. Daniels had been warned before, Gracie watched her sister.

She didn't care. About any of this. In her head, Gracie was sure, Cora thought that this was beneath her. That this man — and anyone else that wanted things from her she was either not willing to give up or didn't care about the consequences of — meant nothing to her. Gracie wondered when her sister had become so horrible.

"She's always been." She looked around, but there was no one speaking to her. "I'm here, on your shoulder. Please don't move so quickly, I'll fall. My name is Othello. We met before, when you were first hurt. I'm a faerie, and yours to use."

"Use how?" Her mom looked at her when she spoke in a whisper, and she explained to her about the faerie. "She said she's mine to use."

"Well, tell her to be quiet or we'll all be in trouble. My goodness, it's hard enough keeping up with this without a little faerie talking too." Mom leaned to look at the little person. "I think I need one of them too. I can think of a great many things I could use one for. I'm looking for someone to help out around the house. And the yard come summer. Then there—"

Her mom seemed to realize she was talking too and turned away. The smile on her face made Gracie think of when she was small and her mom would find the strangest things funny. When Othello began speaking again, telling her to simply listen, Gracie did so.

"Cora has had seventeen lovers that lasted more than a couple of times in bed. There have been many, for shorter periods, but their names are not in her head so I cannot find them. But the boys, as you have been told, they're not her husband's. I don't understand a human that would do that."

142

She asked Othello what she meant. "Have a child by another person that you do not love. And if you think your answers, my lady, I can hear your thoughts. I'm touching your ear now, so I can hear you."

I don't think she ever loved anyone but herself. The little faerie said that might be true as well. *What else do you have to tell me? About my sister? Or something else?*

"Ah yes. She isn't going to have a baby, as you know. She had an infection and they had to remove things when she went in for an abortion a few months back." Gracie turned so quickly that Othello fell off her shoulder and into her lap. "My goodness. It's my fault, but that was scary."

She's had an abortion? She tells anyone that pauses in front of her that she would never do that. Othello shook her head and moved to her shoulder again. *I don't understand.*

"I don't either, my lady, but I do know that she thinks that if everyone believes that she is with child, then she will have people like her more. Her doctor told her that she could not have another child after her abortion because there were complications." Gracie wondered if William knew about that. "He does not know about the loss of the child, I fear. He is as…I think you say, he is as in the dark as you were. But there is no child now, as you know."

Is there more that I should know? Othello told her that there was and that she needed to know some of it now. *All right, but if you're going to drop a bombshell like that one again, hang on tightly.*

"I can do that. My goodness, you are a wonderfully fun master. All right. You have magic. I mean, you were gifted more magic by the king and queen. Not the new ones, but the former ones. I knew them, back when they darkened the skies with their—" Gracie cleared her throat. "Yes, sorry, we'll talk

143

later. You will need to know that a team was put together and went to the house of Bill and his sons as you have requested. We have gathered a great many of their things, toys and such for them."

Thank you. That's very kind of you. But please, don't get yourself into trouble or hurt. Othello said it was their pleasure, and that the children had been so kind to them. *I'm glad that they are. But the house, it's locked up and someone will notice that things are missing.*

"No, my lady, we have taken care of that as well. There are a few items that belong to Bill as well. Things that he touched a great deal, things that were in his heart and head. He is a very sad and lonely man; did you know that?" She said that she did. "He will, as will your mother, be getting a faerie as well. To keep them safe."

My mom will love that, I think. As for Bill, you'll have to have them talk to him. I'm not sure, actually, what he knows of the Bensons other than they're wealthy and kind to him. Othello said that Asher had spoken to him. *Good. That was good of him.*

The trial was moving along now and she watched her sister. Faking a pregnancy wasn't anything new, but it was about the oddest thing her sister had done to date. At least as far as she knew, anyway. Gracie saw the attorney for the courts hand a sheet of paper to Cora's attorney, as well as the judge.

"This is an accounting of all the credit cards and how far in arrears they are. As you can see, Mrs. Daniels had amassed a great deal of debt using them to their maximum limit, and in some cases over the limit. The last payment made on any of them was well over a year ago." The judge put his paperwork down and looked at Cora. "In addition to the credit card debt, there is the household billing, utilities, and the cars."

"What about their home? Is that in arears as well?" The man said that it was a company owned home as of five years ago. "That's not in the paperwork."

"No, sir. It was a private deal that Mr. Daniels got as a perk. When he was promoted, the house was purchased as part of his income. The taxes are up to date for that reason, we believe. But as of his termination, the house no longer is a part of their package and has since been returned to the company. The contents will be sold for restitution for the credit card debt." Judge Brown asked how much that was. "Just over a hundred thousand including the house, which is no longer his but now back to us at a cost."

"You allowed her to charge over a hundred grand on the company cards? How much of it was her husband's debt?"

The man said none, so far as they could tell. All the signatures on the receipts were from Cora Daniels. "That is for one month, sir. The month before, she charged five thousand. That was when our company spoke to her and she said that she'd made a mistake, that it would not happen again. Four days after that conversation, she charged on it again...she bought a sailing boat with it."

"The Marshalls had one and it looked so nice." Everyone stared at Cora when she stood up to justify her purchase. "And it's not like anyone ever used it. I had no idea when I bought it that it was so complicated to use. I just use it to go show off, and to suntan. The water surrounding it is so nice and warm. They can have that for payment if they want. I'll sell it for ten percent more than I—"

"So you knowingly bought a boat with your husband's company card because you wanted to show off?" Cora nodded, grinning like she was glad he understood. "Did you know that you weren't supposed to use the card?"

"Oh yes, but the other cards that I had were all used up, and they wouldn't let me have any more credit on them to get it anyway. And besides, it's not like the company doesn't have the money. Christ, this is the dumbest thing.... When is this going to be done? I've told you before that I want to go home." He told her to sit down. "No, I will not. Just ask me about the things these people are saying and I'll answer them. I really do want to go and see if I can fix this before it hits the papers. Since you won't do this privately I'm going to have a mess to clean up."

"Mrs. Daniels, you have knowingly and willingly stolen from your husband's company. After being told twice not to use the company cards, you did so anyway. There is credit card debt also, that will be years, if ever, before that can be recouped. As well as the time and expense that has to go to trying to get what money they can from hiring people to sell of your things. Have you no remorse?" Cora turned and looked in Gracie's direction. "I'm asking you a question, Mrs. Daniels."

"Gracie will pay it all off. She has money. I was going to talk to her after I got out of here, about her giving me money enough to start over, but now is as good a time as ever. Just go after her. She's a sap." Gracie stood up and stared at her sister. "Tell them that you'll pay this crap off so that I can get out of here. I have no idea how that idiot of a husband you had managed to leave you so well off, but you're not going to spend it so you can just give it to me."

"No." It might have been the first time in her life that telling her sister no didn't make her feel guilty. "I'm not paying her debt, nor will my mom. We've come to the decision that she's made her bed, now she must lie in it."

"Gracie, stop being a dumbass and just tell them that

you'll pay it. You don't need the money anyway. You live like a pauper, and no matter how many times I tell you, you dress like a bum too." Cora looked at the judge. "She was married to this guy who took pictures for a living. Pictures, like anyone cares about that crap when I have some on my cell phone that are nicer. And then he went and killed their only kid. Not that Gracie isn't better off without them. She was never going to be a good mom, not like I am, and I'd have to say that having Cain as her daddy would have mortified any child. Now my sister is shacked up with this other guy that is just as useless and broke. In a months' time, I'm betting that she's broke anyway. She might as well—"

"Enough." No one moved when Onimia stood up and spoke. "You, Cora Daniels, you are a horrible person that does not deserve what you have been given. I cannot believe that you are related to these two women."

"Lord Benson, I had no idea you were related to this... person." Judge Brown stood up and then sat. He looked like he wasn't sure what he was supposed to do now. "I heard that you recently found your other half."

"Her sister." The judge looked at Cora, then at Gracie. "Nothing alike, I'm happy to say. But I believe that we've all heard enough of her lies and opinions. Don't you?"

"What the hell is going on here? What is he in all this?" Cora looked at her and smiled. "You're already having affairs, Gracie? Good for you. But this one, he looks like he might be a bit too much for you. And monied too. Send him my way, why don't you? After you take care of this nasty business."

~~~

Onimia wanted to rip the woman apart, but knew he had to do this like a human, and at the same time, put her into her place so that she never bothered them again. Walking to

147

the front of the courtroom, he was given his way and sat in the witness chair after being sworn in. No one had called him there; he wasn't even sure what he was going to say until he was sitting down. Both attorneys sat in their respective seats and he looked at Judge Brown.

"I'd like to tell you what I've found out. I can assure you, sir, that what I'm about to impart to you, it's the truth. I have...I guess you could say that I have a bit more contacts than anyone here might." Judge Brown asked if there were any objections. When no one denied him, Onimia looked at the packed room. "I've been doing my own bit of investigating over the last several days, and the things that I've found out are much worse than we first thought about Mrs. Daniels."

"Shut up. You have nothing on me." Onimia sat there while Cora screamed at him to get out. To shut his mouth. "Look, perhaps we can come to some kind of arrangements. I'm going to have a baby, but that doesn't mean we can't have fun."

"There is no child." The courtroom was startled to silence. "There never was. The doctors in your hometown have told me that not only can you not have any more children, but that they are treating you for early stages of menopause."

"No. No, that's not right. That's an old woman thing. I'm still young and beautiful." When she was pulled back to her seat, Cora was still yelling, telling everyone that they were wrong.

Onimia turned and looked at Gracie. "She knew that you couldn't have any more and wanted to rub it in your face that she was having her third child. When in fact, she can no longer produce any children due to complications from a sexually transmitted disease they found when she had gone in for an abortion. There was little choice but to sterilize her."

"Why would you do that to me?" Gracie looked at her sister and he could see the pain, the suffering that she was having. He hated to do this, but it was well past time that Cora paid for her misdeeds. "What did I ever do to you that made you hate me so much?"

"Daddy loved you more." He knew this too, that Jimmy Sheppard had loved his second child much more than he did his first. Not that he didn't love Cora, just that he found her to be too much, too much of everything. "He never treated me the way he did you."

"This, all of this, is because you think that? You treated me horribly, my husband and child like they were beneath you, because Daddy loved me more? We were sisters, Cora. I would never have done that to you." Cora said that she would have, if she had let her. "No, I would not have. Ever. Even after all the things you've done and said to me, I still want you to love me."

"Love you? That is never going to happen. I loathe you, Gracie. I hate the very ground that you walk upon, but that does not mean that you're going to get out of getting me out of this situation. You owe me. Everything that I am, it's all ruined because of you." Gracie leaned down and picked up her purse. He thought for sure that she was going to do it, that or pull a gun from her bag and shoot her sister. It was no less than she deserved. But she walked out of the courtroom. "Gracie, get back here right now. I swear to Christ, you're going to pay for this or so help me God, I'll make you suffer. You think that your husband dying was bad? That losing that kid was terrible? You have no idea. I'm never going to let you forget that you owe me. Get back here!"

Onimia watched the woman. She was off her rocker, as his dad would say. She sat down in her seat and looked at him. It was a hard stare, like she was plotting his demise. And the longer she sat there, staring at him, the less he felt sorry for her. Then she stood up and started for the back of the courtroom.

"Mrs. Daniels, we're not finished here." Judge Brown looked at him when she said she'd be right back. "I'm afraid that I can't let you do that. You are still under arrest."

"I'm going to get a gun. I have to make her do this. She's the one that should be in jail, not me. I did nothing wrong and she's — what the fuck do you think you're doing? Unhand me." The officer moved when she did, keeping her from leaving the room. "Get the fuck out of my way and give me that gun. My sister is going to get her ass back here, and she's going to take care of this for me."

"Go back to your seat, miss. I don't want to have to hurt you." The hysteria of the laughter made Onimia's skin crawl. "Miss, you're not helping yourself by being this way."

"You had better not hurt me. I'm going to have a baby and you can't hurt me." She laughed again and turned to look at the front of the room where he was. "Come on, big boy. You and I are going to go get Gracie, and she's going to write me a check. I want to go shopping and other shit on her dime. It's the least she can do."

It took them nearly twenty minutes to wrestle Cora to the ground. She screamed and yelled obscenities at them the entire time, threatening them with everything from killing them to suing them. No one wanted to hurt her...each man that had a hand in keeping her in the courtroom was doing so with her safety in mind, but she had managed to hurt three of the men before anyone could get her cuffed and out of the building.

Onimia walked to Jules and held her as she sobbed on his

shoulder.

"I didn't raise her to be that way. And perhaps her dad did like Gracie more, but it was because Cora didn't make it easy for anyone to love her. She would push them away when they got too close." He said he understood. She looked up at him. "Make my little girl happy, will you, Onimia? She is so loving and wonderful. She needs to be loved more than most women, I think."

"I do love her, Jules, with all my heart. And Gideon and I will make her happy if it's the last thing we do. This I can promise you." She laid her head on his chest again and he held her. "Come on. Gracie is at the diner across the street. Essie and Gideon are with her, but she isn't talking. Come on, she needs us."

Chapter 11

Gracie walked around the big oak before finally sitting down to lean against it. She was exhausted and hadn't been sleeping well. Cora had been tested for her competence and found to be sane. All her insanity, it seemed, was directed at Gracie.

The ground beneath her warmed a little and she smiled. Othello landed on her upright knee.

"I've let the men know that you're with me. They are relieved. You should tell them when you leave the household, my lady. They worry so about you." She said they'd been sleeping and she'd not wanted to wake them. "Still, a note would not have been remiss."

"Thank you, I'll remember that next time." Othello sat down and stared at her. "I'm going to be fine. I've just had a very stressful few days."

"'Tis two weeks since the trial, my lady. You are not getting better." She didn't say anything. Of course she wasn't getting better. She was depressed and hurting. "There is something that I can do for you. I can take your memories of

153

that day."

"No." Othello nodded but didn't say anything. "My memories are what have made me what I am. Not the depressed part of me, but the person that I have become. I knew that my sister didn't like me, I just never knew the extent of her hatred."

"I don't think anyone did." Othello cocked her head, her small ears twitching. "Did you hear that?"

"What?" When she didn't move, neither did Gracie. "My mom is loving her new house. I wanted to thank you for having the faeries go and get it ready for her. And she's fallen in love with having the little ones around. I never knew my mom loved to craft. She has made each of them some furniture that they use at their home."

"She has made me a lovely blanket that I have snuggled under each night for a week. It is most toasty." Gracie said she was making one for their bed at the house too. "I have seen it. The colors are so brilliant, it is like looking at a field of wild flowers."

The noise to her left had her looking. There were several dragons in the woods with them, one a small baby. He was learning to use his fire, she'd been told, and in the trees, it was much easier for him. Gracie wasn't sure how that worked; usually trees and flames wouldn't be something that she thought went together.

"I'm hearing something, perhaps it is the men that circle the dragon lands looking for beasts." She stood up when Othello flew upward. "You will stay here on the property, miss. They cannot harm you here."

Gracie was afraid for the pip. She'd found out the other day, quite by accident, that a group of faeries was called a pip. And a single one was also called a pip. She put her hand

154

on the tree behind her and felt the warmth. When Othello returned, she looked stressed.

"Tell me what it is. Do I need to get the others?" She nodded, then asked her to be calm. "I can't be calm when you ask me to. That's like telling someone not to think of a sneeze, because then that's all you can think about."

"You must remain calm or it will be bad for them." She asked who. "There has been an accident. There are the dead there, needing you."

"You mean, there was just an accident? Have the police gotten there yet?" Othello shook her head. "I'm not going to find some mangled up dead bodies, am—?"

They'd been walking. Gracie hadn't even realized she was being maneuvered until that moment, the moment that a sound brought her to a stop. She knew that sound, and couldn't move.

"I can't do this." Othello said she was the only one that could. "No. You don't understand. I cannot do this. I'll call the others. They can do it."

"If you do not, then she will die." Gracie felt the tears running down her face. She knew what she was going to find if she got any closer to the sound. "Come, my lady. You must help her."

Moving forward, all she could think about was the other time a child had depended on her. That she'd not been able to keep her safe, as she'd promised her the day she'd been born. Failure at her most important job had left her feeling like she would never be able to be there for anyone again.

The crying, as she got closer, sounded like a mewing cat. There was blood everywhere in the deep snow, and she did have a moment of fear. But Othello assured her that she was safe there, the other faeries would make sure of it. Walking to the small pink bundle that had been thrown into the embankment, Gracie felt as if her heart was going to pound out of her chest.

She felt both Gideon and Onimia in her head. There was fear from them, almost as much as she was feeling. Without preamble, she knew they were afraid for her and didn't tease her or ask her nicely why she was no longer in the bed with them.

Where are you? She told Gideon what was going on. *I'm on my way. Onimia is bringing me. Are there others around?*

Dead. She wiped at the tears as she pulled the bundle to her. *I need your mom and sisters. The baby...there's a child, and she's nearly blue with cold.*

Give her to me.

She was surprised to see them there, both her mates. Onimia took the child from her as his dragon and wrapped her into his body and wings. Gracie held onto Gideon.

"He'll be able to warm her up like nothing else will. My family is on their way. Do you know what happened here?" She shook her head. "It's all right, love. I have you now."

The people had been murdered with a knife, or some sort of blade. The cuts to their body were violent, as if they were really pissed off at the people here and had taken their powerful rage out on them. The child, it seemed, had been the only one to survive. At least, Gracie hoped that she would.

The police arrived half an hour later. The baby was doing much better, but still very cold. Essie had brought bottles with her and even tried to nurse the baby, but she was too weak to do much more than cry. They were all worried about her.

"It looks like some of those squatters that you had out here before." Elbert had called the police and told them just what had happened, and that no one, it seemed, had survived but an infant. "I've not called in social services for the baby, Mr. Benson. I was kinda hoping that I could just leave her out of the report. For now, anyway. If someone asks about her, then I'll tell them where she is, but I think she stands a better chance of surviving all this with you people."

"And if we fall head over heels in love with her, what do you expect us to do then? Turn her over to someone that ain't got the sense to come in out of the cold? Do you have any idea what might have happened...? No, not what might have happened, but what would have happened had my Gracie not been out here having herself a little walk? I'll tell you. She wouldn't have been found. That's what would have happened. Some animal would have come along and just had her.... You figure out who these people are and you let me handle them."

Gracie had never seen Jacob so fired up before. She wasn't sure if she thought it was funny or scary, but hugged him when he looked as if he might explode.

Just over his shoulder she could see her...the mother of the little girl. She had no idea why she knew that, but when she came toward her, Gideon and Onimia both stood beside her.

"We came here to find us some dragons." She looked around, then back at them. "Cartwright, he had it in his head that we'd be able to get us a house and such with the kind of money he'd heard them other men talking about."

"What other men? The ones that killed you?" She nodded. "You came out here and they followed you?"

"Oh, it was worse than that. They brought us out here to kill us. My baby? She gonna be all right? When they started chopping on us, I wrapped her up, best I could, and hid her in the snow. I know it was cold, but I didn't want her to die like we were." Gracie told her that she'd saved her life. "You take her for me. Please? We got no family. Not even parents to mourn our deaths. If she gets in the system, like me and Cartwright were, she'll end up spreading her legs for somebody that don't care for her, or at the end of a bullet. You have to take her."

"What's your name? They'll make a search of her family, it's the way the law works." She nodded and stared at the bloodied mess that had been a family, her family. "I can't just take her. There are laws that would protect her."

"His name was Cartwright Smith, and I'm Becky Star. My baby's name is...." She smiled at her and Gracie thought it was beautiful. "I won't tell you her name. You give her something good. Something that she can become. Friendly and wholesome. You do that. But no one will come for her, not anyone, because we weren't people that others would help. We weren't bad, just not worthy of much notice. There ain't no family because we were raised up in a home for motherless children. My baby, she will end up there too if you don't take her."

Gracie didn't tell her that her birth certificate would tell her the name, but nodded at the woman. Doing that seemed to settle her and she turned away. Then when she asked to see the baby, Onimia pulled the blanket from her face and showed her.

"I didn't have her in no hospital. There wasn't any money for such things anyway. There ain't no record of her being birthed. Me and Cartwright, we did it right there in the car." Gracie told her that she'd been lucky. "No, she's the lucky one. You're gonna do right by her. Oh, the men that killed us, they're in town. Staying at the little hotel out on the state route. I saw them about an hour ago. Their names are David

158

and Morris. I don't know the last name of either."

When she walked away, her form getting more and more washed out, Gracie told the officer what she'd found out. If he thought it strange that she could talk to the dead, he didn't act like it. Instead, he smiled at her.

"Congratulations, you got yourself a baby then." Gracie started to tell him that wasn't right, but Gideon thanked him and told him that he'd take care of the paperwork in the morning. "You do that. Thank you for the help on this. It might have been months before we'd be able to piece anything together."

There were officers there now, and no one mentioned the child. They did ask to see her, and were happy that there was another little one in the household, but no one ever assumed that the child was anyone but theirs. Taking her home to get her cleaned up, Gracie was surprised to find Eve waiting for them.

~~~

Eve watched Gracie with the baby. She was terrified of her. And not only that, she seemed to be trying to push it away, not love it. Eve knew why...Gracie was waiting for someone to come and take her from her. When Gideon went into town with Onimia to get supplies, Eve sat with the younger woman.

"She might well have died if you hadn't gone for her." Gracie said nothing, but Eve could feel her heart breaking. "I'm sorry that you are in so much pain, Gracie, but you have a little girl to raise."

"She's not my little girl." The baby stared up at her, her face red from the cold, her little fingers still pink. "They're going to figure this out. Find out that not only does she have nine sisters and brothers, but even grandparents out the ass.

That someone is going to want her."

"There is no one, you know that as well as I." Eve knew that she had to upset the woman, to make her see what was right in front of her, but she didn't want to. There was a great deal at stake here. More than she'd ever dreamed there'd be. "So you'd rather she just would have died out there? Alone and without anyone to comfort her?"

"I should have died." That was the heart of it all, and Eve knew it. "Don't you see? She died because I couldn't protect her. My baby, who didn't hurt anyone in the entire world, died because I wasn't able to save her. What if this one needs me and I can't help her?"

"Did you cause your husband to have an aneurysm? Did you make the car swerve into the oncoming traffic? Did you do everything within your power to save them both? Even going so far as to try and cover Cain with your body when you saw that there was nothing left but for the car to be hit?" Eve stood up and came close to her. "Should you like to see what I see in your memories?"

When Eve filled her body, she saw everything. The conversation they'd had about gifts for their daughter's first Christmas. The things they were going to get Cora and her mom. There was talk of other children, ones that would never be, but mostly it was about their love for one another.

The pain of the aneurysm made him tense up, Gracie asking him if he was all right, then he was gone. Nothing in the world could have kept it from happening at that moment. Cain Hobbs was gone even before his wife finished her question to him.

Gracie thought of her husband, how he'd been her only love. Then of her child. As the impact took her, she shielded him, hoping that someone could save him. Her child, she'd

160

thought, was safe...the car seat she was in was in the right direction, and secure.

But as the baby flew out the front window, her seat still in the back, Gracie witnessed the sight of her little girl being tossed away, her husband, cradled in her arms, already dead. Once the accident was done—the semi had hit fully on her side of the car—she freed herself from the seatbelts and crawled her way to the child.

Beth was gone, her body broken, her skull crushed. There would have been no hope for her either, even if a team of medical professionals had been there. Still Gracie held her, telling her how sorry she was, that she wished she'd done better as a mother. And as grief took her breath away, Eve left her body and sat in front of her.

"I miss her so much every single day. I loved her and Cain with everything that I had. And when they died, I had no one. My mom was in her own grief. My sister, she blamed us both for their deaths, as if we didn't already do that ourselves." Eve told her how sorry she was. "I don't know what to do with this child, Eve. I'm terrified beyond words that I'll mess up again."

"You won't. And I'm going to tell you something that you may not know, but the child became an immortal the moment you touched her. She won't die, Gracie, or leave you. No one will again." Gracie reached up and pulled the little girl to her, holding her while she rocked back and forth for several minutes. "I missed being able to do that. You all gave me such a great gift the other day, to hold our grandchildren, but there is nothing like holding a child to your heart, is there?"

"This will be our only child. Anthony came to tell me that had he been able to, he would have given me the gift of having a child, but there is nothing for him to repair." Gracie didn't ask her, nor was she thinking it, but Eve told her that they'd had nothing to do with the reason for her having a child now. "I know that. I might be really out of it right now, but I know you'd never do such a thing to a baby."

"There will be others. Some of them dragons, others human or other shifters. There is always a need for children to have someone love them when their parents can't or won't. I can guide them here to you." Gracie said she'd have to ask her mates about that. "You do that. In the meantime, I'm going to keep an eye on this little one. I don't think she's quite human. There is a touch of something else within her."

"Wolf." Eve nodded, smelling it now. "Her mom spoke to me again, telling me that while Cartwright was full wolf, she wasn't."

When the men returned, Eve could only stare at the number of things they'd brought home with them. Not only were there diapers and outfits, but they'd gotten Gracie a rocker as well as things that said "Mom" on them. Both of them had tee shirts that said Best Dad, and Eve delighted in watching them hold the baby as if she were the most precious thing in the world to them, and Eve supposed that she was.

"You have a name picked out yet? We need it for her paperwork." Onimia was talking quietly as he fed the child a bottle. "Something strong and proud. Her middle name too. She needs something to live up to."

"Nothing too powerful or weird. You have no idea how much teasing Simeon gets for his name. To us, being born a long time ago, it suits, but nowadays, well, it's not normal to them." Gideon kissed Gracie on the cheek as he walked by her to sit with her on the couch. "She's beautiful, isn't she?"

"Yes. Perhaps the prettiest little wolf I've ever seen." Gideon smiled like he'd been handed a great gift, like a ray of sunshine. "Sunshine. You should name her something to do with the sunshine."

"She's lucky too. There was a name, long ago, that I heard. Fausta. It means fortunate. I think that should be her middle name." They all agreed with Onimia, and then he smiled at her. "Serendipity Fausta Benson. For our luck in having her in our family."

It was settled then; the little girl would be called Serene for short. And they thought that she approved of the name when she yawned and snuggled in her new daddy's arms. After that, Eve made her way back to her cave to tell her love they had another grandchild.

"I missed it. I went to see about the men who had caused the parents' deaths." Eve asked him if they'd been arrested. "No, killed. They resisted and were killed when they fired at the police. Good thing that Asher was in town. I think he was able to save two of the police officers by using the elements around him. Our sons, all of them, they're very good men, aren't they?"

"Yes. You should have seen the things they brought back for the child. It looks as if they might have bought everything there was in the place that even had a bit of pink on it." Anthony wondered if she'd like pink later in life. "I would think that if they keep this up, she'll more than likely grow tired of it." She laid beside him. "Anthony, have you seen anything of our future? Will we be around forever now?"

"I don't know, my love. I wish that I did. I have seen other things. The last mate is on her way. I think she will be the one that completes the magic. Brynhilde will not come easily to them, I think." Eve remembered the woman...she'd been nothing more than a child all those years ago. "She is sure to be a good addition to them, don't you think?"

"She will murder them in their sleep when she figures out what we have done to her." Eve smiled. "She goes by Bryn now, Bryn Scott. Her life has been easier than all the rest, but no less terrifying for her. Do you suppose there are still others out there that hunt for her? Even after all this time?"

"I think that would be a fair statement. To think that we know no more about her now than we did then. I still think she might have been a better match to Asher. 'Tis too late now, but she is hard as nails, and has a temper to match. She is the perfect foil to the last two."

Eve thought of the young woman. She'd been a beauty, even for one so young. Her hair was flaming red, her eyes as green as the land that she'd been sired in. The woman was as Irish as they came, and had every man both afraid of her temper and in awe of her beauty.

"Can you remember what she told me when I asked her for the favor?" Eve laughed when Anthony did. Nodding, she waited for him to continue. "Told me to shove it up my arse. And that if it didn't fit, for me to bend over and she'd pull it from my throat so that I could flap the flavor with my tongue. Even my dragon curled around me then."

"She did agree, in the end." Eve thought of the anger that had Bryn coming to them the day before the big storm. "Anthony, she'll come here, won't she? You don't think she'll back out now that things are coming to a head."

"I have kept an eye on her. She will come here. We really gave her no choice in the matter, love." They hadn't, but it had been close that she'd not. "Simeon and Akassa, they'll need her. More than the others ever did their other halves."

"And we need her as well, to finish the circle. I know that we cannot be with them as Jacob and Sally are, but our time with them will be longer. It will almost be the same." Anthony

164

held her. "I will go and see her in the morning. Just to look at her. I want to get an eye on what she is about, as well as any future grandchildren she might have for us."

"Is six not enough for you for now? My goodness. We have three granddaughters now, and three grandsons." She was glad that he was counting Connor and Mike as their grandchildren.

Chapter 12

After checking on Serene, Gideon made his way back to bed. Onimia was sleeping with his arm around Gracie, and she was wrapped around his pillow. It was a lovely sight to see…the two most important people in his life, holding one another. He got into bed beside Gracie and she wrapped around him.

"She still asleep?" He said that she was fussy for a moment, and he changed her and put her back to bed. "I've never known a baby to sleep all night. Oh, before I forget, she's four months old. Not six like we thought. So that makes her birthday right around the end of July to early August."

"Well find a good day for her to be born on and go from there." Gideon turned so that he was on his back and Gracie over him. "How about you ride me while Onimia suckles at your breasts?" Onimia sat up on the bed and fisted his cock. "Or you could enjoy him while he stands in front of you. You tell us what you want."

They ended up on the floor, Gideon on his back, Gracie on his cock. Onimia stood in front of her, his cock at her mouth while he held his legs. It was the best kind of three way, as far as he was concerned.

As he fucked her, watching her suck on Onimia's cock, Gideon thought himself to be the luckiest man in the world. Lovers that were so generous, a mate that loved them both equally, and a new baby in the other room.

Onimia came before he did. His cum dripping off Gracie's chin made his cock ache to do the same. But when she leaned over him when Onimia moved, he took her mouth as he rolled her to her back and fucked her hard. As soon as her legs wrapped around his hips, Gideon knew that he wasn't going to last long. Screaming out his name, Gracie came three times; each time had her tightening around him so forcefully that he could barely move. But still, it was amazing to him to know that he'd done that for her. And when his own climax took him, Gideon leaned into her throat and bit down hard, drawing on her blood enough that he was dizzy with the flavor.

As soon as he rolled off her, Onimia laid beside them. For now, they were all sated and tired. Holding her between them, Gideon fell into a deep slumber. Tomorrow was going to be a busy day.

The castle was nearly finished with them putting what they could inside. The building itself was talking longer. The magic that had been used from the earth had slowed a great deal due to the winter months and the earth going dormant for a time. Gideon, like the rest of them, hadn't realized how much of the living trees and sunshine that the magic needed to do the last of the work. As it was now, the last turret as well as one entire wall was still being done.

"I'm thinking that come spring this thing will snap into place. What do you think?" He told Asher he wasn't sure.

"You think it might need longer?"

"Longer? No. I think it needs the last mate." Asher looked at the castle, then back at him as Gideon continued. "We're almost complete too...I mean, as families. For some reason, I think that in order for this to be done, as in all the cracks filled and the building as safe as it could be, we all need to be here."

"You might be onto something there. I guess it has been moving along faster with each mate. Gracie brought the end to all the materials and furniture when we were told that would be a few more months longer. Then she shows up and we get the call it's all done." Gideon pointed out that the trees, even though it was winter now, were still producing fruit for the animals. "Yes, not to mention there are more animals being born too."

"Did Simeon tell you that he found someone willing to sell off their horses? I was thinking they'd be a great addition to the place in the back paddock, near the lake." Asher laughed. "What?"

"I thought you were going to tell me that you wanted to feed them to the dragons. I was kinda nervous for a minute there." They both laughed. "But horses, yes that would be a nice touch. And the manure wouldn't be bad either."

As he lifted the large cabinet that was to be put into the living room, Asher helped him carry it in. As soon as they sat it on the floor, magic put it in place against the wall, just to the left of the fireplace. The books that were in a great many boxes on the floor started to lift and put themselves away. All the things like this, books and vases for this room, had been in the lower levels and filled with magic too.

"I have to go into town later. I need to see about a couple of things. I was wondering if you'd come with me." Asher asked him what was going on. "Well, they're going to start jury selection for Cora today. Gracie isn't going to go. She has had enough. I don't think that Jules is either."

"Good. They don't need to hear her spouting her mouth again." Gideon nodded. "Before I forget to tell you, the birth certificate has been filed and you should be getting your copy soon. It has, as you requested, your name as the father, using Onimia as your middle name."

They left for town a bit later. Asher had a list of things he needed to pick up, and while he was there, he was going to see about getting some more help at the castle. Things were moving along now, and they were going to start on the landscaping around it come early spring. No moat, sadly, but there would be a nice sized garden as well as a kitchen garden for the cooks.

"Asher, when we were children, do you ever remembering thinking about getting a mate? And that she'd be for both you and your dragon?" Asher looked like he was thinking on that, so Gideon continued. "We didn't have a lot of contact with the outside world, I know that, but we knew that there was someone out there for us. Right?"

"Oh yeah. I mean, I didn't know then what it would change in our lives, but yes, I would think about her. Of course, back then sex was never a part of that thought process. Mostly it would be about how I'd have to share all my stuff. And even though we had everything that we ever wanted, we didn't really have all that much." Gideon agreed. "What I thought of, when I got older, was how much she was going to change my life. Not in the way that she did, but I guess I thought of all the terrible things she was going to do to me. You never really know until you actually have a mate what will happen, but I love Essie, with all my heart and soul. And having a child with her? That's like having all the cake and icing too.

170

Why do you ask?"

"Gracie is going through some really hard times right now. I guess she had a talk with Eve yesterday, and that seemed to bring her out of most of the depression, but she's afraid of messing up with Serene." Asher said he could understand that. "Yeah, me too. But I worry for her. She's not herself."

"She'll be fine. It's going to take her a little while." Gideon hoped so. He missed the old Gracie. "Perhaps she needs this time alone with the baby. You know, to understand that she can do this."

"That's what Onimia said too. He's at the castle today, and I'm running errands I'd rather not be doing. You're to keep me away until after dinner." Asher said he'd do that for him. "I have a list of things I'm to pick up too. And as far as Serene, I'm not to purchase anything that isn't on this list. She was very firm on that."

They were still laughing when they entered the mall, and Asher led him right to the baby store. Well, led might not have been entirely correct, but they did spend a lot of time there, as well as a couple of other places that primarily dealt with babies. By the time they were leaving, several trips to the car had been necessary. Even Asher had gone a little overboard. Not that either of them minded, but they were having fun.

"You're a bad influence. And don't think I don't know what you're doing. Making me buy so that you don't have to look bad to your wife." Gideon didn't even try to deny it. "What the hell were we thinking? We're going to be in so much trouble. We'll need to buy our wives something, just to be sure we don't get our heads bashed in."

"Excellent idea. I love the way your mind works." It took them a while to pick out the perfect gift for their mates, and then longer still to get something for their mom. It was fun,

171

hanging out with his brother, and Gideon decided that he'd try to do it more often.

It was well past dinner when they started home. The most grueling part of the day had been sitting in the courtroom while people were picked as jurors. But it had been worth it, just to be with his brother for the rest of the day.

They'd gotten everything they were told to, as well as a great many extras. But for him, it had been better for the company. He'd not realized how much he needed to just to be a brother and friend for a little while. When he entered the house, quietly because there wasn't much sound, he saw Gracie asleep in the rocker that had been his mom's, with little Serene sound asleep in her arms. Onimia was sitting across from them, watching.

You should have been here earlier. I think things are going to be fine now. My mom came and had a talk with her. Gideon nodded. *They're beautiful, don't you think? I mean, I love them both as if she were my own child.*

It's been taken care of…she is our child. Onimia nodded and got up. *I got some things in the truck if you want to help me bring them in.*

I do. Did you go overboard? Gideon nodded, with a smile that hurt his face. *Good. I wish I could have been there with you too. I love having a mate and child. It is much better than I ever dreamed it would be.*

It might have taken them less time to bring things in, but they had a blast going through each of the bags they'd brought in. By the time Gracie joined them, not only did she join them, but since the baby was awake, they had a mini fashion show too. Gideon was still laughing when they went up to bed later that night.

~~~

Jules sat on the deck with her tea and watched the dragons. Here she was, she thought, sitting in a lovely home in the middle of nowhere enjoying life again, while watching dragons playing in the field beyond. Taking a sip of the brew, she smiled when Wednesday joined her.

"I have good news for you, my lady." Jules didn't bother telling the little brownie that she wasn't a lady, but asked her what her news was. "There are two more babies coming today. The dragons will have a celebration, and you have been invited. You have come to mean a great deal to the dragons, and they all wish you there when their own child is hatched as well."

Three days ago Jules had been taking a long walk in the forest when she came upon a small dragon. Well, she'd not known it was a dragon when she rushed in to help it, but she was glad that she didn't know then. Had she, Jules wasn't sure that she would have gone any closer. But the female did need her help.

They couldn't communicate. The dragon was in distress, she could see that, and something, Jules had no idea what, made her trust her. Sitting on her knees in front of the beautiful mother, she looked down at that egg that was having trouble opening.

There was a small crack in the top of the beautiful egg, and the point of a little nose peeked from it. The egg was varying shades of green. Jules found out later that was so it could stay hidden in the grass when necessary. But this egg, it wasn't opening easily, and the little dragon was exhausted trying to free himself. The mother, with her first babe, wasn't sure what to do either.

Jules wanted to just bust it open, and help the little baby out, but she wasn't sure that was what was needed.

Instead, she simply reached in and rubbed the head of the dragon that she could see…she supposed to give it some sort of encouragement. But what scared her nearly to death was being knocked away. Not by the momma, but she supposed the daddy.

The female roared at the male when she leapt at him. There was a small fight that ended with the female blowing flames at the male and sending him on his way. When she settled back by her egg, she pulled Jules closer and nodded. Touching the tiny head again, she started nervous talking. More like terrified talking, but it soothed them both.

"I guess I never realized that dragons had eggs. Well, I guess that makes sense now, but since I never thought about it, I assumed you had baby dragons. Who would have thought that there were even any dragons around anymore? Your baby is pretty. Since I can't tell its sex from here, I'm saying pretty." She looked at the momma when she clicked. "You're talking to me?"

The sound was like that of Morse code…a series of clicking noises that seemed to be in a pattern. Jules had no idea, but another large hunk of the egg broke away, the little guy spilled out on the ground and laid there.

"My goodness, look at him. He's so handsome." The sound behind her had her turning slowly, fearful of the male returning. Jules tried to shield the dragon and mother from whatever came after them, and decided right then that she'd die before anyone touched them. But it was Lindsey, and she was smiling at her. "We've had a baby dragon."

"Yes, she told me. She said that you saved her child's life by being here." Jules told her she wasn't so sure about all that. "To her, you did. And she's very proud that you were the first human she's seen that didn't want to murder her or her child."

"I don't think her mate is all that thrilled about me." The baby started to stand and stumbled into her lap. Jules helped him to stand, then rubbed her fingers over his head. The small spike caught her finger, and before she could put the small wound to her mouth, the little dragon licked it. "He isn't going to want more, is he?"

Lindsey laughed. "No. He's now a part of you and you him. Forevermore, he will be your champion." Jules asked what that meant. "He has a little of your blood. From now on, he'll be there to save you should you need it. That's a great gift you've been given."

And now she had been called upon to go to three more hatchings, that's what they were called, to be there when they were brought into the world. A good omen, Lindsey had called her. The other dragons felt the same way about her. So, she had a job of sorts. And was paid in a way that made her one of the richest women she knew...with diamonds made from tears of joy. She had no idea what their worth was, but she saved them, for the pure joy of them being given to her as a gift of friendship and love.

"Wednesday, have you seen my daughter today? I was wondering how she was doing." She was told that she was doing very well and that her mates were home. "I'm glad. She seems so lost without them."

"As it should be, my lady. When you find yourself a mate, things will be the same with you." She didn't bother telling her that her mate was gone and that she had no desire nor heart left enough to give to someone else. "Shall I tell the others that you would gladly join them in the hatching? I think there is going to be a small celebration as well. You will need to be there for that too. This is a wonderful honor you hold now. Mother of Dragons, they're calling you."

"Yes. I'll be there. But this time I'm walking. Tell them not to send a dragon to get me unless it's close to the time the babies come into the world." She shivered when she thought of her ride yesterday in the claws of a large dragon. "I prefer to fly in planes, not soaring through the air exposed like that again. While I was there in plenty of time, I was still terrified out of my mind with worry that I was going to be dropped on my head."

Wednesday was still laughing when she left her. As she sat there, just enjoying life, she thought of her husband. Jimmy would have loved this. He would have been flying all over the place with the dragons, and inspecting every part of them for the joy of it. He was a man who had enjoyed life to the fullest. And she missed that about him most of all. She could almost hear him now.

"Jules, my love, you need to expand your horizons more. Get out there and see what this is all about." He would smile at her, his face alight with humor and good thoughts. "Ah, my angel, you are the best thing that has ever happened to these dragons, and they know it."

She missed him with every beat of her heart and breath that she took that didn't have his scent with it. Jimmy had been the reason that her heart beat and that she lived. If it hadn't been for Gracie needing her, she was sure that she might have joined him.

"Hello." Jules found herself sitting up straighter in her chair and wiping quickly at the tears on her cheeks. "You're going to be all right; you know that, don't you?"

"Am I?" She nodded at Sally to join her on the porch when she asked. "I've not been dealing as well as I had hoped. Well, I had hoped that I'd be spending the rest of my life with my husband, but he got sick and died. I know that it's been a few years, but I feel it as if it only happened this morning."

"Yes, I heard. I'm so sorry for your loss. I have been with Jacob for nearly as long as there has been grass on that mountain over there. There are days when I wish to bash his head in, and others when I think I can't be without him another moment. Of late, the bashing has been winning out. I'd forgotten how he's like a dog with a bone about things. And for all his professed thinking that he's a modern man, he's as stuck in the past as I am." Jules laughed when she did. "You're a wonderful person. I was thinking about you this morn. You have taken this, all of this going on around you, very well for a human. Few would have been so good about having dragons and such around them all the time. And the magic here as well. I'm very proud to call you a friend."

"Yes, so I've been told. Wednesday said that I was her favorite human. That's not really saying a great deal since I'm the only one she knows. But I think of you as a friend as well. And I thank you for being so welcoming to me. After Cora, I fully expected to be turned out on my ear. I didn't realize how.... Well, she's a horrible person, and I'm glad that she's getting her just rewards." Gobi and Caroline joined them on the porch, chairs appearing as they sat down into them. "Oh, to be so magic that I'd not have to worry about where to place my bottom when I'm resting."

"You have magic, my dear. You were gifted it when you helped with the first baby hatchling coming into his world." A knitting needle and yarn appeared in Gobi's hands as she spoke. "I think it's only a wee bit, but you could make yourself whatever you wish. Go on now, have a go at it."

"Go at what?" Caroline asked her what she wanted. "A Danish, with cream cheese and cherries so fat that they defy reason."

She'd been thinking about it for several days, since she'd seen the scones that one of the girls was making. And Elbert... boy oh boy, that man could whip up a batch of the best smelling and tasting things she'd ever seen or smelled. The plate of them appeared in front of her, on a larger table that hadn't been there before. Jules looked at the three women.

"You did it." Sally reached for one and it changed to blueberries before she bit into it. "I prefer these to cherries. I love them, but I like blueberries better. Oh, this is very good."

Nodding, Jules tried to ignore the weird feeling in her belly. She'd made Danishes and they were being eaten. Trying to convince herself that one of the other three women had done it, she knew, deep in her heart, that she'd actually had enough magic to make them. Smiling a little, she picked up her tea cup with shaking hands.

"Yesterday when I was having a soak in the tub, I wished for warmer water and the water did get warmer. Today when I was baking something for lunch, I simply thought of having a cup of tea and it appeared in front of me." Setting down her cup, she stared at it as she continued. "I tried to tell myself that it was in my head, that the water wasn't all that cooled in the first place, and I'd made the cup and had forgotten about it. But I did it, didn't I?"

"You did, yes, and quite brilliantly too. I talked to your daughter today. She's doing much better with the child. And Serene will be such a joy to her from now on. I think, however, that she's taken the boys to task. They've been shopping, and have brought home a great many things that are too old for her." Sally laughed as she continued. "Yesterday Gracie told them if they brought home one more item she was going to put the baby under a rock and leave it there for the faeries to hide away. I think they believed her, because I've not see a single empty box laying near the trashcan since."

"When I spoke to her last evening, she told me that one of them had the idea to buy her a car. I laughed until I was nearly sick with it. A car, for a child." Jules felt her love for the baby to her bones. "Gracie will be a good momma. And today I get to see the boys for a little while. Bill is going to work and they're coming to stay with me."

"Oh, how wonderful. You should join us then. We're going to go shopping in town for some Christmas things. And with Thanksgiving only a few days out, we're in need of some other items." Jules admitted that she'd not been in the mood to celebrate the holidays much anymore. "You will this year. We have so many grandchildren now that we'll have to have a big tree and all the trimmings. You must see the way the faeries decorate. I wonder if they still do that here for them."

"I've been thinking I should go and see Cora." Sally nodded, as did Caroline. "The trial for her is soon. I'm not sure yet why she's in jail over credit card debt, but perhaps it's the best place for her. She can't harm herself there. Not that I think she'd kill herself, but she can be a bit on the obnoxious side, and someone else might just want her hurt."

"She's in trouble with a great many people, according to what they've been able to find out. The contents of the house are to be sold in a few days, and it is my understanding that Gracie is going to go and find a few more things for the boys. Bill has expressed no desire for anything, as it is too painful for him." Jules had heard that as well. "The faeries and brownies have been finding items in the house for them and bringing them to them. Clothing and such. There were a few pictures as well, mostly for young Mike. Those poor boys."

"Yes. Connor is a bit clingy, and I let him be. His brother

179

is somewhat angry, but he's getting over that with the help of Gideon and Onimia. They've been helping him work through it by showing him how to use a sword. Mark, he has one as well." Jules thought of the heritage of young Mark. His father had been a dragon slayer. "These people here, they're an odd sort of grouping, aren't they?"

"Oh my yes." Caroline laughed as she continued. "You'd think we were a circus coming to town. But thankfully, we're all safe here. And that is what matters more than anything."

Yes, safe. It was a word that Jules had never thought of herself as needing. Safety. But here, with this land and these people, she felt that, all the way to her feet. Knowing that for as long as she lived, she'd not have to worry about anything other than what she was going to try today. It was a wonderful feeling.

Chapter 13

Cora sat on the bench and looked up at the sun. She was going to jail. That much she did know. It was the why that she couldn't figure out. It was just a little bit of debt. William had a good job. He could just work a little more overtime, she'd try and cut back on her spending, and things would work out. There wasn't any reason for her to be put in jail. They were out to get her, that's all it was. People hated successful people like her.

"Hello, Cora." She didn't even turn towards the sound of her mother's voice. That was another person she wasn't happy with right now. "I've come to see you. Aren't you even going to speak to me?"

"Do you have anything nice to say to me? If not, then go away. I have had enough people telling me what a terrible person I've been." Mother asked her who had done that. "That person who thinks he's going to marry my sister."

"They're married, and he loves her." Cora snorted. "You don't think he loves her, or is it that you don't think he should love her?"

"I don't care what anyone thinks about me." Her mother said that wasn't what she had asked her. "There is no such thing as love. William didn't love me any more than I loved him. And Gracie isn't like me. She'll just fall in and out of love like a yo-yo."

"I don't even know what you're talking about. Look at me, Cora. I want to talk to you about your sons." Cora turned to her mother and noticed that she was dressed very nicely. That she'd even had her nails and hair done. Cora asked her about it. "I was shopping with some friends. We got thing for the kids for Christmas, and some things for—"

"Why didn't you use that money to buy me out of here? I swear, Mother, you can be so selfish sometimes. I'm sitting in here, without family or friends, and you're out having a good time without me. Not that I'd take you shopping with me—you're just not into the same sort of things I am—but really. What were you thinking?" Her mother laughed and Cora stared at her. "What is wrong with you?"

"Nothing. Not a damned thing. My goodness, Cora, how did you become such a selfish bitch? It certainly wasn't me or your father. Nor did Gracie have anything to do with—"

"Do not talk to me about Gracie. She isn't my sister any more. Did you know that she has money? A great deal of it? Who would have thought that she'd be the one with all the cash, while I sit here in prison without even a robe or soaps of my own? I was supposed to be the one with it all. Not her. She married some deadbeat that didn't have shit. Now look at her. And she keeps rubbing it in my face." Mother asked her if she believed that, that Gracie was rubbing it in her face. "I do. I really do. She's got money, and she won't even give enough of it to me to get me out of this mess. This is all her fault. I shouldn't be in here. It should have been her."

182

"Why would you say such a thing? Gracie has lost so much. Her husband. Her child." Cora pointed out that she'd not have any of her money without a dead family. "Cora. What a thing to say about your own sister."

"It's not like she has any idea what to do with it. I mean, seriously, she's as stupid now about money as she was when we were children. Why on earth would she not have spent any of it by now? I mean, I would have." Cora didn't understand how she'd been born to this family. They were all insane. Her mother laughed again and Cora hated the sound of it. "I'm betting she has it hidden under her mattress, and counts it every night to make sure that the mice haven't gotten to it. What a stupid twit she is, Mother. And you're not much better. Selling your house when I'm going to have to drive further to use you as a sitter. When I get out of here, things are going to be different, I can tell you that."

"Yes, and look where it has landed you having it all. Even going so far as to spending money that you had no rights to. And I've sold my house. Just today, as a matter of fact. The furniture has been brought to me and I have a lovely home. Your sister's house is going to be rented out, for couples that might need a start. You should be proud of her, not pissed off all the time." Cora told her that she didn't care about what Gracie was doing. "Why not? You're not a nice person, as I'm sure people have been telling you. You made it so that your husband lost his job. That he has to pay back all the money that you took from his company by way of giving up some of his retirement. Cora, that was wrong of you, and I'm sure that you know it."

"He's my husband, that's what he's supposed to do." She looked at her mother when she snorted. "You've been the worst mother to me. I hope you know that. When Gracie

183

needed you, you left me without a sitter and ran to her side. Never me, did you?"

"Cora, I don't think that leaving you without a sitter so that you could go out to lunch with your friends is equal to your sister losing her husband and child and nearly dying herself." Cora turned away from her. "She's happy now. You should be happy for her too. She has a little girl now that she and her husband adopted, and they're doing well."

"I hate her. I have for a very long time." Mother told her to stop that. "It's the truth. And you too, to be honest. You were never a good mother. You thought I was a terrible person because I had a good life. Money. Friends. I don't want you to come here again. And when I get out, I'm going to get my children and husband and we're going to go far away from you. I'll only call you when I'm desperate for a sitter."

"Don't bother." She turned away from her mother; this was what she wanted, to be begged to stay. "Don't bother calling me when you get out, even if you're desperate. The children aren't going to go with you when you get out, nor will Bill. He's moved on, and the children, for the first time since I've known them, are happy and thriving. They're in a good school, with other children to play with. They have grandparents in Sally and Jacob that love them as much as I do. You should really try calling your so-called friends, Cora. See which of them will come running to your side. I'm betting none of them will."

Cora wasn't going to speak to her mother now. Not until she spoke first. She could do it too…Cora was known for her ability to not talk to someone for hours on end, even while being in the same room with them. When time seemed to come to a standstill, the sun moving across the cold sky, she thought she'd have a look to see how badly she'd hurt her mother. To see her crying quietly would be just the thing to cheer her up.

But she was gone. Cora stood up to see that not only was her mother gone, but the footprints from her walk out to see Cora, as well as the ones from her walk back, were already filled in with the snow that had started to fall. Cora realized that she was all alone. Not just here, but all alone in the world.

When her time was up to be out of doors, she made her way back into the building. She'd not told her mom, but she'd called her friends. Three women who had been with her through all the shopping sprees. The luncheons at the club, as well as when she was depressed or bored. Cora had come to enjoy their company as much as she thought they had hers, but it had been lies. All of it.

"Are you kidding me right now, Cora? You want me to drop everything and come to see you? In a jail cell? No, I don't think so. I don't swing that way."

She'd made three more phone calls over the next few days. Not only did she get refused, but one of them actually told her that it was where she belonged. Apparently, she'd found out about her having an affair with her husband. Did no one keep secrets any longer? So here she was, without anyone to complain to, and her family was being mean to her. It just wasn't fair. Not at all.

Cora hated her life right now. Everything about it was all messed up. She wanted it to be the way it had been, before her sister and mother had intruded in on her life. And here she was, the prize of the family, in a jail cell for no other reason than she wanted things to be pretty. Life sucked.

~~~

Bryn moved through the throng of people and tried not to cringe when they bumped against her. People, humans, were a horrid bunch for the most part. And the few that weren't out only to serve themselves were too young to know that they'd grow to be monsters as well.

The child darted in front of her just as the car moved forward. "Christ." The magic that she rarely used surged forth, and Bryn snatched up the child and moved it to the sidewalk before the car could smash it to the pavement. As soon as the kid was settled, Bryn looked for its mother. The stupid twit had her face buried in her phone, and her eyes not on what they should have been. Bryn was tempted to smash her with the car, but decided there was enough death in this world without her contributing to it.

Moving forward, she saw the woman before she spotted her. Bryn moved to the building that was behind her and blended into the brick. There wasn't anywhere else for her to go. To run would alert her, to stand out in the open would get her killed. Just as she was ready to blast the woman, she moved past her with her eyes forever searching. Bryn stayed where she was for several more minutes, just to make sure that she wasn't going to be found.

Few could see her for what she was. A faerie of considerable magic, Bryn had been sought after for centuries…since she was a small child, she supposed. Now, while there were few who came after her, they were more determined than ever to have her as part of their magic. As a war faerie, Bryn would fight for whoever owned her. And it mattered little what her opinion of the war might be.

The woman, a queen of something so mundane as a bunch of vampires, wanted her to watch their kiss during the day. To fight off anyone that came to end them, and to make sure that when they woke there was food for them all. It wasn't a job that she wanted. However, if caught and claimed, she'd have to do whatever was told to her, and there wasn't anything she could do about it. Not even to kill her master or herself.

When the woman was gone, she made her way to the apartment building where she lived. The place that she was staying was a dump for all appearances, but inside, where she was alone and without the fear of being caught, she had things looking like she wanted them. Magic was plentiful for someone of her age, and she didn't like to live in squander.

There was much more room inside her little home than it looked from the outside. And, because of the magic, she was able to let her outer body go and become herself. The real Bryn, the feared Brynhilde of centuries ago.

"My lady?" Tinsel looked the same as he had all those years ago, when he'd first come to her to help her hide. As bland as a person could be, in direct opposite of his name, Tinsel would appear in shades of brown and white, no other color but that. But he'd been her only constant, as well as only friend, all these years. "You had two visitors today. One of them slipped a pamphlet under the door—I have taken it to the rubbish bin—and there was someone calling out to see you. Not by name, but he called you Warrior."

"Did you see what he looked like?" Tinsel said he'd only heard his voice, fearful of going into the hall to see him. "Good. I don't want you caught either. There are things going on here that will make it so that we must move on soon. Not to mention, I have that thing to do for the former king. The tricky bastard."

"Yes, he was most trickier." She smiled at him and he flushed. "I know not what that means, tricky. I have looked for the word, but the definition is as confusing as the word is itself."

"It means that he did something underhanded. Not really,

I suppose. I did agree to do it, but dangling food in front of a starving child wasn't very nice of him." Tinsel said that it hadn't been nice at all. "We'll have to go back there soon. I have the book that goes to the man called Asher. He is the son of Jacob and Sally. Remember them? No matter; he would be about ready for it, I guess."

"Yes. You said that you were to wait until the castle was near complete before going. Do you think that it is?" She told him that she knew that it was nearly so, that she could feel the magic of it. "We should go before the man returns. It is mostly dangerous here with him slurping about the corners."

She loved the little guy. But there were times when she wished that he got out more. He was forever saying things that took her several minutes to figure out what he was saying. Today was no different. But this time she didn't correct him. It was just too much effort, and she was exhausted. Lying on her hammock, Bryn rocked back and forth gently. There was a soft breeze blowing over her, as well as the scent of roses. When Tinsel landed on her knee, she started to ask him what he wanted for dinner, when pounding on the door made them both suit up.

"Warrior? I know that you're here. I have followed your scent, and I know that you reside here." Nodding to Tinsel, she had him go to the wall and pull their things together. "Warrior, I wish to have you."

The bag that held the book was there, as well as money and identifications for herself. Tinsel could and would be anything she needed him to be, mostly decorations on her clothing, but he would also, with his own magic, be able to hide away a great many things for them both. The little guy could easily carry her in his magical pocket should it become necessary. She hoped it never came to that.

"Go to the building. You remember it?" He nodded, his wings fluttering quickly at his back. "Don't come back here. Even if I'm late coming to you. I might have to take care of something else."

"Yes, mistress. I shall wait until you come." She nodded and lifted her hand to snap her fingers. "Mistress, please do not let him capture you. All will be lost should you do that."

"Lost?" He nodded. "I don't understand. We have everything we ever need. What do you think we should lose?"

Before he could answer, if he was going to, the pounding started again. With a snap of her fingers, Tinsel was gone with all their supplies. Turning to the door, she lifted her arms above her head and closed her eyes. Magic coursed through her body at just a thought.

The room shifted and changed to what it had originally been. The walls warped and paper peeled off. The floors were no longer covered in the finest of rugs, but now covered in filthy and droppings from rodents. The plants, all of them of a tropical nature, disappeared, their origins never to be known to anyone of this century or country.

As the room began to change, so did she. Her armor shifted with her weapons. She was covered from head to toe with a shield so thick and so hard that nothing could penetrate it. Bryn felt her hair grow, lengthening to her knees and then beyond. Its rich red color would be so bright that it would tell anyone looking at her that she was Irish. Even her eyes, she knew, would darken to a green so deep that it would be wondered if she could see from them. As her room finished so did her true self.

The door exploded open, no longer strong enough without her magic to keep it closed. The man standing here, also in armor, would be no match for her under normal circumstances, but he held a child in his arms, one that lived in the building with her. The man held his blade to the child's throat as if he meant to embed it into his small neck.

"You know nothing about me if you think the murder of a small child will detour me." She stared at the man as a drip of blood flowed down the neck of the kid. "He isn't human."

It was almost too fast. The dragon in front of the man shifted so quickly that she nearly missed her opportunity to lash out to save herself. Even though she was able to remove both their heads, she was hurt, and badly too, if the pain was any indication.

She moved to the portal, the one that she'd made for Tinsel, and called out to him. Her blood was staining the floor, her head spinning from it. And even though she was immortal, she could still be drained by losing too much. Bryn would need to rest for several days, if not longer, to make herself strong again.

"You have done it this time, my lady. Yes indebted, you have done it now." She told him to gather what he could of the dragon. Tinsel collected everything that the dragon had left them, which was a bounty when she thought of what someone would willingly give for it. "I shall stash this away, then deal with you. Should anyone come upon this or feel his demise, we will be hunted more than we are now."

"Just hurry. I'm in pain and fading fast." He said that he was and she closed her eyes. The small touch of his fingers to her face had her staring up at him. "I'm going to need to go into hiding now."

"To the house of the dragon king." She nodded, sure that if anyone could help her, it would be him. After all, she'd been told he was going to be the greatest, even above Anthony. "I shall take us there. You won't enjoy the trip, I fear."

"It matters little, I think. Once we have finished his assignment to us, we can go on that long vacation we said we would. No more dragon slayers after us." He nodded, but she could see the fear in his eyes. "What is it, Tinsel? Am I hurt worse than I think?"

"I doubt that, but you are hurt badly. I fear that once you are with the man at the castle, you will not be any more pleased than you are now." She asked him what he meant. "The dragon king, he has picked you for his son."

"Son? He has no son." Tinsel nodded, her head dizzy with his movement. "Tell me what you know or so help me, I'll turn you into a collar and stick you to a dog's ear. One that has many ticks and bugs."

"King Anthony bid me come to see him. Just after he spoke to you. He said for me to keep you safe, that you were the mate to one of his sons. He has six, it is mine to understand." Nodding, Bryn didn't care for where this was going. "King Anthony told me that someday you would take the book to the man, Asher, and hand it over. When you were there, you would meet the man that is to be your heart. He and another man, I do not know his name."

"Two men are to share me? I don't think so. You must have heard him wrong. Or remembered it incorrectly." Tinsel said that was possible, but there was a mate for her. "I don't need a mate, Tinsel. You know that I'd just as soon kill a man than to have him too close. I like my solitude."

"Your solitude-ness is done for, my lady. You have a mate. I shall take you there now, and you can mend while getting to know them." Bryn told him no, that she'd rather go into hiding. "You will be, in hiding, I mean, but your mate is awaiting you. You must go."

The magic took her breath away and she felt herself being

folded up with it. She'd be a speck now, nothing more than a piece of lint in a human's pocket in size and shape. But the only place she would be, after this, was with Tinsel. And he'd be to the king of dragons before she could get her wits about her. As the blood loss took her under, all she could think about was that she'd been betrayed.

The ride was smooth and quiet. She knew that Tinsel thought he was doing the right thing, and with the king telling him to do this, he would have had no choice but to do as he told him. Keeping it from her, however, after the king was dead, had been the wrong thing to do. They were friends, good friends, and he had sold her out.

As soon as she felt the magic, that of the new king, she made her way out of Tinsel's pocket. He'd not know it, of course, as he was so committed to his task. As soon as she felt the air around her shift and change, Bryn shifted to a bird before being blown away and made her way to the trees to rest. The blood loss was great now, and she knew that she only had a few minutes to get herself to safety and away from the man or men who would take her.

As a warrior faerie she would have no choice in the matter should he claim her. It was something that she had dreaded her entire life. To be claimed by anyone. It had, over the years, happened to her many times.

A few hundred years ago she'd been taken and made a slave. Not sexually, that was never allowed to be, but she was to fight his wars, most that he brought upon himself, and to win. When she lost, for any reason, she would have to forfeit herself. Either her long life of being his slave with her sword or her body. So far no one had claimed either, thankfully. But a mate would be different.

He would demand her allegiance. Not only with her

heart, but her sword too. Bryn had seen what a mate could do to one of her kind. It was neither pretty nor romantic. She had been lucky until now, and she planned on staying that way.

The large structure caught her attention just as she was dropping from the sky. Her bird landed badly…since she was already weak, it was as well. Hopping to the highest point on the thing, she realized that it was an old barn, one that hadn't been in use for a very long time. Going inside, careful where she tread, she found some straw that wasn't in too bad of shape and dug herself a hole to hide in. Bryn knew it would be days before she'd be able to move again, and figured that the deeper she was, the better off she'd be. She was much too weak before she was able to make herself secure in the building. But she did know that no one would find her. Bryn closed her eyes just as the sun was coming up over the mountain.

Chapter 14

The early morning sunshine looked beautiful over the snow. Gracie had just put Serene down for her mid-morning nap when she heard one of the men coming down the stairs. Smiling at Gideon, she asked him if he wanted any breakfast.

"I do, and you're perfect for what I have in mind." Before she could tell him that the baby was in the next room, he had dropped to his knees in front of her and was eating her pussy. Holding onto the wall behind her, she nearly fainted when Onimia came into the room, naked and hard, his hand wrapped tightly around his cock.

"I heard there was breakfast to be feasted upon." She couldn't have told him no if her life depended on it. "I love finding you here, with your pussy being eaten. You have no idea how long that memory stays with me all day."

Her gown was pulled off her and he was at her breasts, suckling hard and loud while he rubbed his cock over her thigh. Gideon was moaning now, his mouth doing all kinds of amazing things to her, and she knew that when she came, they'd change places with each other.

"I'm going to come like this." Onimia said he certainly hoped so. "Please, you have to come with me, both of you. I need to feel you both."

Gideon stood up and held her while she steadied on her feet. When she was ready, he led her to the table where Onimia was sitting, his cock thick with need. Leaning over him, she took him in her mouth just as Gideon slammed into her pussy from behind. It was the most wonderful feeling in the world, having both their cocks inside of her.

She sucked on Onimia hard, fondling his balls, making him moan and cry out when she gave them a gentle but firm twist. When Gideon leaned over her, cupping her breasts in his hands, she held onto Onimia while she was fucked harder.

"Lean back." She did as she was told and felt the first hot spray hit her in the belly. Even as Onimia came on her, she could feel Gideon filling her pussy. She was ready to beg them to give her some relief when she was spread on the table and Gideon climbed over her. As he fucked her breasts, Onimia ate her.

Gracie came four times while they switched around on her body. She was exhausted and sated by the time they were ready for more. Gracie loved her mates, more than she thought would have ever been possible.

The shower was their favorite place, she supposed, next to the bedroom, and while she stood holding onto the tile wall, they scrubbed and nibbled on every inch of her. By the time she came out of the bathroom, she could barely move and Serene was awake.

"I'll get her." Onimia loved holding their daughter, and did so whenever he could. Not to spoil her, but he talked to her, about anything and everything. "I'll bring her in here and we can nap together. There isn't any castle work today, being

196

Thanksgiving."

The celebration was set for two, and she was sure that Sally and Elbert had been up well before dawn to start cooking. She'd volunteered to help, but was told that Sally had missed so many of these dinners that she wanted the cooking for herself. The men were setting up the table, but the rest was Sally's to do.

Serene snuggled between her and Onimia when she was brought back, and she stared at them all. She was a beautiful little girl. Her hair had yet to show any kind of color, just a golden patch of fuzz at the back of her head. Her eyes, however, were the deepest shade of amethyst that she'd ever seen. Onimia had said that it made her seem older than she was, like she was the new body of an old and powerful soul. She thought he might be right.

When she woke, she was alone in the big bed. Stretching out some of the kinks that she'd gotten from all the sex, she smiled as she made her way to the shower. It was going to be a great day. There was going to be plenty of good food and better company.

Dressing in her warm clothing, she was headed over to the big house when she saw Othello. When she landed on the doorknob in front of her, Gracie asked after the baby. Then the men and the rest of the family.

"They are well, my lady. But we have a visitor. And he is most upset." She asked why she came to her. "He feels that his mistress is in her rest mode."

"I don't know what that means. Rest mode? Is she a vampire?" She told her she was not. "Then how am I to find her when she'd not dead? I'm assuming that's why you came here."

"She is a faerie...a warrior faerie." That didn't help her

197

and she told her that. "She is an immortal, same as us, but she has been around for far longer than even Elbert. She was a friend of the former king and queen. Well, not friend so much as a warrior for them. They thought her a child, but she was older then than the—"

"Othello, please. Tell me why you're upset about this warrior faerie. I mean, how much harm can she do to a bunch of dragons that live here?" Othello told her that she had killed one recently. "Does Asher know?"

"No, my lady. He knows nothing. But her brownie wishes to speak to you. He said that he wants you to warm the path. I don't know what that means, but that is what he said." Othello looked confused. "What is it, this warm the path?"

"I don't know, but I have an idea he wants me to go ahead of him for some reason. And if this warrior killed a dragon, which I'm assuming is a tiny one, then I don't know what he thinks I can do." Othello looked at her with an odd expression. "How big is this faerie, the warrior?"

"Big. Like you big." Oh, well that changed things. "She is very powerful and old. She would know better than to kill a dragon too. She was told to come here now by the king and queen. Tinsel, her brownie, said that she is set to be a mate to the former king's child. It would be Akassa, correct?"

"Yes, that would be my guess too since he's the only one not mated." She tried to think what she needed to do to make this happen for all of them. "This brownie, his name is Tinsel? Like you'd put on a tree?"

Again the odd look, so she explained what that was as well. "You wish to have metal on your tree? We use things from the forest. It is most beautiful. But should you want some metal, we can find some for you."

"No, that's all right. I meant that.... You know, it doesn't matter. Have the little guy come here and I'll see what his story is." She said she would tell him now. "And Othello, if I miss even one minute of Thanksgiving, I'm not going to be very happy."

When the little man showed up, it took her ten minutes to get him to stop bowing before her. Then another five for the story. It seemed that the lady in question had run from him because she had found out about her mate being here. Then he went on to explain about how her services were given to whomever trapped her.

"So, in order for her to come here, I'm going to have to trap her? I don't think so. For some reason, the word warrior with her name is sort of off putting, don't you think? I mean, I'd like to keep all my limbs for a bit longer." The brownie looked at the trees, then at her. "Not tree limbs, but.... Christ this is going to take forever. Is she in danger, this faerie?"

"No, my lady. I shouldn't think so. So long as she is resting, there is no one looking for her. Unless they followed her to her hiding place. Which I don't know where that might be. She ran from my pocket." Gracie asked how big she was. "Now? I know not. When I last saw her, she was in my pocket, as a speck."

Gracie rubbed her forehead and wondered if she was going to need an x-ray or something after this. Her head was hurting badly enough that she wanted to go back to bed. As the little man argued with Othello, she tried to think, but it was too hard with all the noise. So putting her finger into her mouth, she whistled.

Both of them looked at her with the strangest expression. She wondered if anyone had whistled at them before, and decided that she'd keep that in mind when things were getting out of hand. And she was sure that they would. Gracie stood there for several minutes, gathering her thoughts and making a plan she could work with.

"All right. I'll go and talk to Asher for you. I don't know what he's going to say or want, but I'm assuming that he'll want to see this warrior." Tinsel nodded and started to speak when she put up her hand. "No more for the moment please. I want you to go with me...not that I think anyone is going to understand you any more than I do, but they might. And for that I will be eternally grateful. After that, we'll have to see what goes from here. All right?"

"I don't know." Neither did she, but that was fine. They were all stabbing in the dark here. "I shall go and find her, my lady, if you don't mind."

"I do mind, actually. If she's resting, then we can find her better. If you startle her or make her aware that we're looking for her, then she'll run. This way is better for everyone." She hoped so at least. "Now, we're going to see Asher."

As she walked across the path to the big house, she wondered about the warrior and how she would fit in with the rest of them. Gracie had no idea what a warrior faerie was, but it sounded like a great title. But the size of her, how she was a speck in a pocket of a person only about two inches tall, and big like her too. It was going to be something she looked up, if there was a book that had anything like this in it.

Gracie opened the door and walked right into Asher. He had a baby in each arm and both were crying. She took one as she explained what was going on.

"Warrior faeries are all gone." She told him apparently not. "What I meant was, I've not heard of one being around for more years than I can remember there being any. What did he say she was doing here?"

"I didn't get a chance to ask other than she's mate to

Simeon. And I would assume Akassa. How does that work, with her slaying dragons?" He said he had no idea, but he'd find out. "Oh, and she's hurt. I don't know how badly, but she's gone into some sort of sleep to heal."

"Hibernate." She asked him if he was making that up. "No. It's really what she is doing. Hibernating so that she can shut down her body to heal. Where is she?"

"I don't know, and neither does Tinsel." He asked about the name. "Yeah, I was shocked by that too. Tinsel. And don't mention it around any of the other faeries or brownies. You'll have to take an hour out of your day trying to explain why you want metal on your tree."

~~~

Simeon wasn't sure he was going to be able to sit down with his family. His mate, their mate, was close to them, and she was hurt. He didn't know what had happened as yet, other than she'd killed a dragon in self-defense, nor did he know how badly it had hurt her when she did it. Apparently too, she was being hunted. Something else to worry over. Simeon looked at Akassa when he said his name.

"She is here, our mate, she's here." Simeon nodded, playing with the food on his plate. "You'll need to eat more. If she is indeed a warrior faerie, she'll need us to be stronger for her when she comes to us."

"Do you know anything about her kind?" Akassa said he knew very little, but Elbert knew a great deal. "We should sit down with him then, find out what she's going to need in the way of medicines and food."

"That's not what I meant when I said she'd need you stronger." Simeon looked at Akassa, then it hit him. "See, you are smarter than average. You know as well as I that sex between mates is intense and very involved."

201

KATHI S. BARTON

"I don't care for you right now." Akassa laughed. "Look, we'll just enjoy our dinner with the family, then go out and see if we can find her. That way we can bring her here and make sure that she's all right."

"Just what part of warrior faerie did you not get?" Simeon was going to go home. He'd had enough of being the butt of jokes. "She's in better shape than we'll ever be, even hurt as she is, but we will go looking. Perhaps we can have sex with her while we're out there."

"You are a sick individual; did you know that?" Akassa was still laughing when they were to clear the table of dinner so that dessert could be brought in. "I don't want you sitting next to me. I might be tempted to hit you."

He wouldn't, of course. His mom would knock his head back, and he'd be made to wash up the dishes on his own. Not a fun time when it was such a big holiday. As it was, they were all going to be a couple of hours on clean up. Simeon sat at the table with his family and looked around. This time next year, he'd have a mate, and maybe a child. Suddenly finding his mate didn't seem so scary.

Before You Go...

HELP AN AUTHOR

write a review

THANK YOU!

Share your voice and help guide other readers to these wonderful books. Even if it's only a line or two your reviews help readers discover the author's books so they can continue creating stories that you'll love. Login to your favorite retailer and leave a review. Thank you.

Kathi Barton, winner of the Pinnacle Book Achievement award as well as a best-selling author on Amazon and All Romance books, lives in Nashport, Ohio with her husband Paul. When not creating new worlds and romance, Kathi and her husband enjoy camping and going to auctions. She can also be seen at county fairs with her husband who is an artist and potter.

Her muse, a cross between Jimmy Stewart and Hugh Jackman, brings her stories to life for her readers in a way that has them coming back time and again for more. Her favorite genre is paranormal romance with a great deal of spice. You can visit Kathi online and drop her an email if you'd like. She loves hearing from her fans. aaronskiss@gmail.com.

Follow Kathi on her blog: http://kathisbartonauthor.blogspot.com/

www.ingramcontent.com/pod-product-compliance
Lightning Source LLC
Chambersburg PA
CBHW032129170626
46808CB00006B/2155